PANHANDLE JUSTICE
THE CROCKETTS' WESTERN SAGA: 5

ROBERT VAUGHAN

WOLFPACK
PUBLISHING
— EST 2013 —

Published in the United States by Wolfpack Publishing, Las Vegas

Wolfpack Publishing
5130 S. Fort Apache Road, 215-380
Las Vegas, NV 89148

wolfpackpublishing.com

Paperback ISBN 978-1-64734-789-5
eBook ISBN 978-1-64734-788-8

PANHANDLE JUSTICE

Chapter One

A heavy, booming thunder rolled over the breaks and gray veils of rain hung down from ominous black clouds that crowded the hills. Though it had not yet reached them, the storm was moving quickly, and Will and Gid Crockett took ponchos from their saddlebags and slipped them on to be prepared for the impending downpour.

Will was about five feet, eight inches tall, ash-blond, young in years, but with the hard face and the seasoned blue eyes of someone who had seen more than his due of hard times. Gid was six feet one with broad shoulders and darker hair. But if anyone ever doubted that he and Will were brothers, they had only to look into Gid's eyes, for they were the duplicate of Will's, and they measured life with the same reserved scrutiny.

"Will!" Gid called to his older brother. "We need to find us a place to get to!"

"You think we're made of sugar, Little Brother?" Will teased. "You afraid we're goin' to melt if we get wet?"

"We won't melt, but we're goin' to be damn uncomfortable," Gid growled.

"Well, what do you say we head toward that ridge over there?" Will suggested, pointing to a long red escarpment. "Maybe we'll find an overhang to get under."

"Yeah, good idea."

The two riders broke just to the right of the trail they had been following, and the horses, perhaps anticipating the shelter of the ridge, quickened their pace without being urged to do so.

Will and Gid Crockett were in the Texas Panhandle, having arrived there in a casual westward drift that neither proposed a particular destination nor had a sense of purpose. The brothers hailed from Missouri, but years of bloody border war as members of Quantrill's Raiders had set them on their wandering. Their wartime activity had earned them a degree of notoriety and, like Frank and Jesse James, the Younger brothers, and others who had ridden with them during the late war, they had once been regarded as outlaws and their pictures had been on reward posters in Missouri, Kansas, Arkansas, Louisiana, and even in parts of Texas.

At the end of the Civil War millions of soldiers who had worn the blue and the gray lay down their arms and picked up where they had left off. Friendships were renewed, crops were put in, men and women were married, children were born, and their lives went on as if nothing had happened.

But it was not to be so for all men. For some the wounds had cut too deeply and the price had been too dear. Families, fortunes, and dreams were consumed in flames and drowned in blood. Will and Gid were such men. They had only each other, a dwindling number of their peers, their guns, their courage, and a peculiar, though quite rigid code of honor to sustain them. For them the war had not ended. Only the battles had changed.

As they got closer to their destination they saw a small, man-made structure of rock, adobe, and wood, clinging to the base of the cliff. A wisp of smoke was curling up from the chimney.

"Look," Gid said. "There's a cabin, and someone is in it."

"Yeah, I see it."

"Do you think whoever it is will be neighborly? It sure would be nice to dry out by a fire."

"We'll never know till we try."

They started toward the small cabin, just as the rain hit. The rain fell steadily, the big drops drumming against the ponchos, pooling, then sliding off. To the west, streaks of lightning slashed down from the dark clouds, and thunder boomed and roared. The horses, with no way to shelter themselves, occasionally shook their heads to keep the water from running into their eyes. Their manes lay wet and heavy on the sides of their necks.

When they came within hailing distance of the cabin, Will held up his hand and started to call out, but before he could do so, a puff of smoke erupted from the window, followed by the sound of a rifle shot. A singing bullet took off his hat.

"Hey! Hold on there!" Will shouted. "We don't mean you—"

The rifle fired a second time, this time hitting Gid's horse. The animal, struck in the heart, went down so quickly that Gid just barely managed to leap clear.

"Stop shooting, you son of a bitch!" Will shouted. He leaped down from his own horse, snaked the rifle from his saddle holster, then slapped the animal on the rump to get it out of the way. "Gid, you all right?" he called.

"Yeah," Gid said.

A third bullet hit the ground just beside Will, kicking up water, mud, and gravel before whining off into the valley behind him. Bending over at the waist, Will ran toward Gid, then dived for cover behind the dead horse. Gid had already done the same thing.

"What kind of fool would just open up on a couple of strangers for no reason?" Gid asked.

"I don't know," Will said. "But whoever, and whatever

he is, he surely has the advantage."

"Hey in there," Gid called. "What are you shootin' at us for? We mean you no harm."

There was no answer.

"You reckon the son of a bitch can't speak English?" Gid asked.

"Could be," Will agreed. "Maybe he'll understand this." Will fished a white handkerchief from his pocket and tied it onto the end of the rifle barrel.

"What the hell? We goin' to surrender to him?"

"Not surrendering, Little Brother," Will said. "I'm trying to get him to agree to a parley. I figure if we can get him to talk to us, we can convince him we're not his enemy."

Will raised the white flag and began waving it back and forth. Another shot rang out from the cabin, and the bullet hit the horse not two inches away from Will.

"That does it," Will said angrily, jacking a round into the chamber of his rifle. He rolled over onto his stomach, raised up slightly, and, resting the rifle across the body of Gid's horse, took a long, careful aim at the window. He waited and watched, and when he saw the shooter's rifle barrel come out of the window again, he aimed just to the right of it and squeezed the trigger.

The shooter in the cabin dropped his rifle, and it tumbled to the porch. An arm fell out as well and hung down motionless on the outside of the window.

"You got 'im!" Gid said.

"Yeah, I think so," Will replied. He continued to look, cautiously, toward the house. "If he was the only one."

The two brothers lay in the pouring rain for another four or five minutes, closely studying the house, which was approximately thirty-five yards away.

"He must've been the only one there," Gid finally said. "I think we should go in and get out of the rain."

"Wait," Will cautioned. "Impatience can get you killed."

"So can pneumonia, which we're going to get if we stay out here in this rain long enough," Gid growled.

Will raised up cautiously and looked toward the house. When no one shot at him, he stood. Gid stood with him.

"Let's go in," Will said. He cocked his rifle, and the two brothers started toward the front door of the cabin.

As they approached the cabin, Will took a look around. To the left of the cabin, tucked up under the overhang of a rock, he saw two horses standing stoically in a small corral.

"There has to be two of them in there," Will said, holding up two fingers. "There are two horses."

"How come we haven't heard from the other one?" Gid asked.

"I don't know. But I think we'd better spread out a little," Will suggested. The two brothers separated themselves by several feet, while continuing their approach toward the cabin.

As they got closer to the house Will could see that the window through which their assailant had been shooting was casement style, and it was opened out, onto the porch. The shooter's arm hung down toward the porch, and Will could see that a tiny streak of blood had run down his arm and pooled onto the floor beneath his hand. When hit, the shooter had fallen against the wall just under the window.

Will approached the house from one side, Gid from the other. Signaling each other, the two brothers stepped up onto the porch, the roof of which was supported by narrow pillars. Staying close to the wall and keeping their eyes on the window in case someone else suddenly appeared, they moved cautiously toward the front door, coming from the opposite ends of the porch. Finally they reached it.

"I'll bust it open," Gid whispered. "You be ready."

Will put the rifle down and leaned it against the front wall. He pulled his pistol, pointed it toward the front door, cocked it, then looked at Gid and nodded.

Of the two brothers, Gid, though younger, was forty pounds heavier and much stronger. Using his shoulder as a battering ram, he crashed into the door. The door popped open and Gid fell to the floor, then rolled quickly to one side. Will rushed in behind him, his pistol in his hand, ready, if need be, to do battle.

No one challenged them.

Will stayed where he was for a long moment. He looked, cautiously, around the cabin, but he saw no one else. Then he went over to the window and, bending over the man who had been shooting at them, pulled him away from the wall. The shooter was a fairly small man with dirty brown hair, sun-browned, leathery skin, a hawklike nose, and a drooping moustache. There was a black hole in his forehead, the entry wound of the bullet from Will's rifle. One of the shooter's eyes was open, the other was half shut. Both had already taken on the opaque dullness of death.

"You drilled him dead center," Gid said.

"Yeah," Will agreed. He sighed as he put his pistol away. "It didn't have to be that way. Why did he shoot at us?"

Gid shrugged. "Who knows?" he asked. "Could be that he was out here alone for so long that he just plumb went loco."

"I reckon so," Will said. "Don't like killin' folks for no reason, though."

"You had a reason, Big Brother. Same reason we had for killin' men during the war. He was tryin' to kill us."

A very close lightning bolt, followed immediately by thunder, caused both men to jump and look toward the window. Gid laughed.

"See what I mean?" Gid said. "We just got here, and already a little thunderstorm has us jumpy."

"Well, at least we're out of the rain," Will said. He stood at the open casement window and looked out across the valley at the rain. He looked in the direction from which he and Gid had just come and realized that the shooter had enjoyed the advantage of being able to see them for several minutes before they arrived.

"Look here," Will said, pointing toward the valley. "There's no excuse for him shooting at us. He had plenty of time to watch us come up on him. He wouldn't have had to look too hard to see that we meant him no harm."

"The son of a bitch planned to kill us," Gid said. "And he would have, if he had been a better shot."

"You're right. I just don't know why he wanted to," Will agreed.

Gid looked around the cabin, then on the far side of the room he saw the source of the smoke they had seen, a small, wood-burning stove. "Hey, maybe he's got something to eat," he suggested. "I'll have a look."

Will remained by the window as his brother went over to the other side of the cabin, to the little area that served as the kitchen.

"What the hell?" he heard Gid gasp.

Will turned quickly away from the window. "What is it?" he asked.

13

"Will, maybe you'd better get over here."

Pulling his pistol, Will stepped quickly across the room until he was standing beside his brother. Seeing the flabbergasted expression on Gid's face, he looked in the same direction Gid was looking.

There on the floor, unnoticed by their first glance around, and looking up at them with large, frightened, deep blue eyes, was one of the most beautiful women Will had ever seen. She made no sound, because she couldn't. She was gagged, and she was bound, hands and feet.

She was also totally naked.

Chapter Two

"Thank God!" the woman said as soon as the gag was removed.

"Are you all right?" Will asked as he untied her wrists.

"No, I'm not all right," the woman answered, gasping for breath and rubbing her wrists. "You found me bound and gagged and naked. Did that seem all right to you?" The woman spoke with a very cultured accent that Will found particularly pleasing. He even appreciated the fact that her tone was more angry than whimpering.

"What I meant was, have you been ... uh, did they harm you in any way?"

"I wasn't raped, if that's what you mean," the woman said. "And I wasn't beaten. But I have been here, in this deplorable and humiliating state, for three days. My clothes are in the corner over there. Would you please get them for me?"

"Gid," Will said. Gid, who had been standing by, un-abashedly looking on, nodded then retrieved her clothes.

"You will forgive me for not playing the role of the shy maiden," the woman said. "But having been kept in this state for nearly a week and not knowing whether I was to live or die, a little thing like modesty seemed unimportant. However, now that the immediate danger has passed, perhaps you two would be so kind as to offer me your backsides?"

"What?" Gid asked, confused by the woman's accent and speech patterns.

The woman made a little circular motion with her hand. "Would you turn around, please?"

"Sorry, miss," Will replied as he and Gid turned around. "We had no intention of making you feel uncomfortable."

"No apology necessary. You saved my life; I doubt that you could do anything now that would render me uncomfortable. Did my father send you after me?"

"No, ma'am, we don't know who your pa is. Who are you, and how did you come to be in such a predicament?"

"My father is Sir Robin Westbury. Knowing who he is, I'm sure you can imagine what they wanted with me. I am Victoria Westbury. You may turn around now."

"I'm afraid that still doesn't tell us too much," Will said.

The woman looked at them in surprise. "You mean you've never heard of my father? Or of Camelot?"

"Camelot?"

"My father's ranch."

Will shook his head. "No, ma'am. My brother and I aren't from around here."

"Oh, how vain I must've sounded to you just then," she said. Her hair was in total disarray, and she tried to push it back. Then, pulling bits of straw and lint from her hair, she examined it in her fingers. "Oh, my God, look at this," she said. She looked around the room. "I'm glad there isn't a looking glass about. If I could see how I looked now, I would really be humiliated."

"How you look?" Will said. He smiled. "Well, you're a mite mussed, I'll grant you that. But I don't know as I've ever seen a prettier woman in my whole life."

Victoria laughed. "I'll take that as a compliment," she said.

"I've never heard a woman talk like you do before," Gid said. "Not even a Yankee."

"That's because I'm not a Yankee," Victoria said. "I'm English."

"You're from England? What are you doing in Texas?"

"Look, can we discuss this later?" Victoria asked. "There were four of them when I was taken. The other three rode off yesterday. I should like to be gone before they get back."

They waited another half an hour for the storm to pass before they left. By now Will's horse, which he had slapped on the rump to get away from the firefight, had returned and was standing quietly just outside the cabin. The two horses in the corral provided the other mounts they needed. One was the horse Victoria had been riding when she was abducted, the other had belonged to the shooter. Gid took that horse to replace the one the shooter had killed. Then, with Victoria pointing out the direction, they rode away, splashing through the shimmering pools of water that remained from the recent rain.

To the north, yellow and gray foothills climbed up to red buttes, guarded over by ring-tailed hawks that sailed along the walls, their sharp eyes searching for prey. To the south lay heavily timbered ridgelines, rich with the smell of sage and pine, and thickly populated by squawking blue jays and bounding deer.

Sensing that Victoria wanted to ride in silence for a while, Will didn't ask her anything until nearly dusk. Then he asked about her father's ranch.

"It is called Camelot," Victoria answered.

"Camelot. Seems to me like I've heard that before," Will said. "Isn't that the name of the castle where King Arthur lived?"

"Yes, but Camelot was much more than just a castle and the town where he lived. It was a state of being, a symbol of truth and beauty," Victoria answered. "And father feels that way about the ranch. It's more than the sum total of sixty thousand acres of grasslands, purple mountains, crystal waters, two score cowboys, and thirty thousand head of cattle. It is my father's American dream, and, like King Arthur's Camelot, my father's ranch is a magical kingdom."

Gid heard none of Victoria's poetry. He heard only the hard numbers. "Sixty thousand acres?" he replied. "Damn! That's a hell of a big place." He recalled the six hundred acres his family farmed before the war. It had been considered large, for the area. He could barely imagine 60,000 acres.

"Camelot sounds like quite a place," Will said.

"It is," Victoria insisted.

They rode for the rest of the afternoon in comparative silence, then, locating a place with ample wood and a good supply of water and grass for the horses, they decided to make camp for the night.

Half an hour later they had a fire going, coffee boiling, and a freshly killed rabbit turning on a spit. Gid hobbled the horses and turned them out where they could reach water and grass.

"I hope you like rabbit," Will said. "I'm sure you are used to far grander meals."

"I'll not complain," Victoria said as she leaned back

against a rock and stretched her legs out in front of her. "Though if you don't mind, I'll take water with my rabbit, rather than coffee."

"You don't drink coffee?" Will asked in surprise. "How can you not drink coffee?"

Victoria chuckled. "I'm fascinated by you Americans and your coffee. That seems to be your main staple. I much prefer tea."

"Sorry that we can't offer you any tea," Will said. "But we do have a good supply of fresh water here."

Gid, who had left camp a few minutes earlier to "have a look around," came back now to join them. "I found a spot for the lookout," he said. "We'll be high enough to have a good view in all directions, but we won't stand out against the sky."

"Good," Will said.

"Lookout?" Victoria said.

"If those other three men came back and found their friend dead today, they are already on our trail," Will said.

"Oh, I hadn't thought of that," Victoria said, putting her hand to her mouth. "Now I've put you two in danger as well."

Will chuckled. "We've been in danger before," he said.

"I'm sure you have been," Victoria said. "Were you in the war?"

"Yes."

"The war was over before my father and I came to this country. In fact, you might say it was the war that brought us here, or rather, the depressed land prices caused by the war. But I have read about it, and I have heard others talk of it. I know that there were unspeakable horrors during the war. I assume that you and your brother fought for the Confederacy?"

"We fought with Quantrill for Missouri," Will said. "And we fought for each other. We didn't give much thought to the Confederacy, but seeing as we fought against Federal troops from the North, I guess you could say we were Rebels."

"Quantrill? I... I believe I have heard of him."

"What have you heard?"

"That he was a murderer and despoiler of women and children," Victoria said. "Surely, you and your brother didn't ally yourselves with such a man?"

"Ally ourselves with such a man?" Will replied. He shook his head. "Don't you understand, Miss Westbury? We *are* such men."

"But surely you are not, sir. Otherwise, you wouldn't have rescued me." Suddenly she gasped, as if coming to a realization. "Unless you *haven't* rescued me, but have merely replaced my captors. Is that the case?"

Neither Will nor Gid answered her question, and she looked at them anxiously as Gid tested the rabbit with his knife, declared it done, then cut it into serving sizes and lay it out on a flat rock. He opened a little pouch of salt and sprinkled it on the meat, then stepped back.

Though she was hungry, Victoria held back until she was invited.

"Thank you," she mumbled, taking a piece of the meat then sitting back down, keeping a wary eye on her two rescuers ... if indeed that was what they were.

"I'll take the first watch," Gid said, taking some of the meat and a cup of coffee with him.

Will unrolled his bedroll beside a rock, then looked over at Victoria.

"You can sleep here," he said. "I'll use Gid's blankets. We won't be sleeping at the same time, anyway."

"You haven't answered my question," Victoria said.

"What question?"

"Have you become my captors?"

"Is that what you think?"

"I... I don't know what to think. By your own admission you and your brother rode for Quantrill."

"And that means what? That we don't quite come up to your image of Knights of the Round Table, rescuing fair damsels from dragons?" Will said.

"You might say that," Victoria admitted, surprised by Will's reference.

Will sighed. "We are not your captors, Miss Westbury,"

he said. He pointed toward the darkness. "You are free to go now, if you wish."

"No," Victoria said. "I'm sorry I questioned you. I would prefer to stay, if you don't mind."

"You may stay," Will said.

Victoria smiled. "Thank you," she said. "And I'm sorry I questioned you."

"That's all right," Will said. "But I suggest you get some sleep now."

"Good idea," Victoria said, pulling the blanket over her shoulders and closing her eyes.

Will laid out Gid's blanket as well, then, taking off his boots and unbuckling his gun belt, he crawled into the bed.

It seemed like only moments later that Gid was shaking him gently.

"Time already? All right, I'm getting up," Will said, reaching for his boots.

"It's not that," Gid hissed. "We've got company comin'."

Will was instantly awake. "How far?" he asked.

" 'Bout a mile back down the trail," Gid said. "I saw 'em first when one of 'em lit up a pipe. And the moon is shinin' so bright that I was able to see 'em again when they forded the river. There are three of 'em."

"If there are three, then it must be them," Victoria said,

having been awakened by Gid and Will's whispering. Her voice was touched with fear.

"You want to saddle up and ride on?" Gid asked.

Will stroked his chin for a minute and thought, then shook his head.

"No," he said. "Let's make 'em do what we want them to do. Throw some more wood on the campfire. Let's get it going well."

"The campfire? But won't that lead them right to us?" Victoria asked.

"That's what I'm counting on," Will replied.

When the campfire was built up, Will and Gid brought in some pine boughs to cover with the blankets, thus providing silhouettes for the bedrolls. Then, quietly, Will, Gid, and Victoria moved about twenty yards to the west, behind a rock outcropping. There, they waited.

Victoria was with Will, Gid was about fifteen yards south of them. The three men trailing would be approaching from the east.

Victoria reached over to put her hand on him. It was a move designed to calm her own fears; she just needed to know that she wasn't here alone.

Will heard something in the dark. "Shh," he hissed quietly.

They sat there silently, with Will's gaze sweeping back and forth, looking for any movement in the dark. He had learned long ago that his night vision worked better by not looking directly at an object, but by looking off to one side. He didn't know why that was, but it was a technique that he had used frequently and he was using it now.

From somewhere out in the darkness a small pebble was dislodged. Will felt, rather than heard, Victoria stiffen beside him, and he knew that she had heard it too. He reached over to touch her reassuringly, and also as a caution to remain quiet.

According to the position of the stars, Will knew that it was now about midnight. If Gid hadn't awakened him earlier, he would have been waking him now anyway.

Will remained very still and looked around slowly, still not concentrating on any one spot. Using this sweeping technique, he detected movement, silent shadows slipping through the darkness. He saw two, then the third.

The three men moved on into the camp where they stood, guns drawn, in the glow of the fire. One of them, obviously the leader of the three, held up his finger to get the attention of the other two. He pointed to the sleeping rolls where Will and Gid had put their boots. It was obviously their intention to kill whoever had come for Victoria, then take her back with them. The three men pointed their guns at the two sleeping rolls.

"Now!" the leader of the three shouted, and he fired first. The other two fired immediately afterward, the muzzle flashes of their pistols lighting up the night.

Will stood up and fired, using the twelve-inch wide muzzle blast of one of the shooters as his target. When he opened up, Gid did as well. All three assailants were hit in the opening fusillade, and though they tried to return fire, their efforts had no more effect than to add to the pulses of light that were now emanating from Will's and Gid's guns.

Had anyone within a distance of several miles been witness to the event, they would have reported a series of lightning flashes, for indeed, that is what they were. The trees and rocks were illuminated in bursts of stark white and featureless black, and Victoria watched with horrid fascination as the three assailants' faces contorted in pain and shock.

The shooting stopped, though the sounds of the last reports continued to echo back from the steep side of a distant mesa. Finally even the echoes played out, and absolute silence returned.

"Gid," Will called out to his brother. When he didn't get an answer he called again, with a bit more urgency. "Gid? You all right?"

"Yeah," Gid answered, his voice right on top of them now, for he had walked back to join Will and Victoria. "I'm all right. How about you two?"

"We're fine," Will said. He looked over at Victoria, who,

though uninjured, was still in a state of semi-shock. "Did you get a look at them?" he asked.

Victoria nodded, but she said nothing.

"Are they the same ones who took you?"

"I think so. I didn't get that good a look at them."

"How about taking a good look now?"

Victoria shivered. "Do I have to?"

"I know it won't be pleasant," Will said. "But we need to know if these are the same ones. If one of them is different, that means there could still be someone out there after you."

Victoria nodded, then she stuck her hand out toward Will, asking silently that he take hold of it. He did, and leading her gently through the rocks, they walked to look down upon the three corpses. Two were already on their backs, the third was facedown. Will turned him over. Squeezing Will's hand, Victoria studied the faces.

"Yes," she finally said. "Those are the ones who were in the cabin."

"What do we do with them now?" Gid asked.

"Leave them," Will said. "We'll move our camp about a mile on down the road."

"Thanks," Victoria said. "I wasn't looking forward to spending another night with them around ... even if they are dead."

Chapter Three

Neither Will nor Gid had ever seen anything like it back in Missouri. The house was huge, with cupolas, and dormers, and so many windows that the morning sun flashed back in such brilliance that it almost looked as if the house were on fire.

The house reminded Will of a wedding cake he had once seen, white and tiered. And not just the house. Even the surrounding lawn was built up in a series of terraces, which worked up from the road to the base of the house itself. A large, white-graveled driveway made a U in front of the house where a coach and four sat at the ready, its highly polished paint job glistening in the morning sun. A crest of some sort was on the door of the coach.

Will and Gid stopped at an intricately carved oak hitching rail, then slid down from their saddles and tied off their horses. Will helped Victoria down.

As they started toward the broad steps leading up to the front porch, the front door suddenly opened, and two men came out, carrying rifles. The rifles were pointed at Gid and Will.

"Put your hands up and let my daughter go!" one of the men shouted, staring down the barrel of his rifle.

"Father, no!" Victoria shouted quickly. "These gentlemen aren't my abductors. They are my rescuers."

The man who had challenged them, a tall, broad-shouldered man with a full head of snow-white hair, raised his head and allowed the end of his rifle to lower.

"What's that? Your rescuers, you say?"

"Yes, Father. They found me and brought me back safely."

"Burton, lower your piece," the man ordered, setting his own rifle down and leaning it against the front wall of the house.

"Very good, sir," Burton replied. Burton was wearing a starched shirt, with paper collar, a tie, and a cutaway jacket. Victoria's father was wearing denim trousers and a plain white shirt. Smiling, he came down the steps with his arms spread wide, smothering his daughter in a bearlike embrace.

"Thank God you have been safely returned to me," he said. "I have nearly every hand out looking for you, and I've notified the sheriffs in three counties. I posted a reward—" He stopped in mid-sentence and looked at Will and Gid. "The reward, I nearly forgot. But, of course, that is yours now."

"Mr. Westbury, we didn't bring her back for a reward," Will said. "We didn't even know about it."

"You didn't know about it? How could you not know? I put the word out everywhere."

"We just rode into this part of the country," Will said.

"Father, they didn't know who I was when they found me. And they had never even heard of you."

"Never heard of me? My word," Westbury said. "Well, that is certainly bruising to one's ego."

Victoria laughed. "A little ego deflation is good for you," she said. "Otherwise, it might get so big that the entire state of Texas couldn't hold it."

"Yes, well, it doesn't matter," Westbury said. "The important thing is you have been brought home, none the worse for wear." Suddenly he stopped and stared intensely at her for a long moment. "You *are* none the worse for wear, aren't you, my dear? I mean ... uh, you weren't..." He let the question hang, unfinished.

"I'm fine, Father," Victoria said quickly. "I wasn't defiled."

Westbury cleared his throat in embarrassment. "That doesn't change anything. As soon as those blackguards are found, I shall see to it that they are brought to justice."

"It's a little late for that," Will said.

"Late? What do you mean? It's never too late."

"What he means, Father, is that the four men who did this have already been brought to justice."

"They're in jail?" Westbury asked.

"They're dead," Will said.

"Dead?"

"My brother and I killed them."

"My word," Westbury said. "You two men don't pussyfoot around, do you?"

"Pussyfoot around?" Will repeated. He laughed. "No, I reckon you might say we don't do that."

"Where are my manners?" Westbury asked. He extended his hand. "My name is Westbury, Robin J. Westbury. And you two are ... ?"

"I'm Will Crockett. This is my brother, Gid," Will said, shaking Westbury's hand. Gid shook it next.

"Well, Mr. Will and Mr. Gid Crockett, it doesn't matter whether you knew about the reward or not, it is yours to claim, nevertheless," Westbury said. "I offered five thousand dollars to whoever would bring my daughter back to me, unharmed, and you two have done so. Therefore, the money is yours. That is, unless you have some aversion to money."

"No, Mr. Westbury, we don't have an aversion to money," Will said.

"Ah, good, then you will take it," Westbury said. "If you will wait right here, I'll get it for you."

"Father, we can do more than that," Victoria said, stopping her father as he started back up the steps. Westbury looked over at her.

"You have something else in mind?" he asked.

Victoria smiled up at Will. "I thought you might at least invite them to have lunch with us," she suggested.

"Yes, of course," Westbury replied quickly. "I would, indeed, be honored if you would stay for lunch." He pointed toward the bunkhouse. "You can clean up in there, if you would like."

Will chuckled. "Mr. Westbury, we accept your invitation, but you've never seen my brother eat. He can put a serious dent in your supplies."

Westbury laughed heartily. "Not to worry, my boy," he said. "We're having beef, and since there are more than thirty thousand of the creatures on the place, I expect there'll be enough." He pointed to the barn. "You can unsaddle your horses and turn them loose in there until you are ready for them again. They'll find plenty of food and water."

"Thanks," Will said.

An hour later Will and Gid returned to the main house. They had washed at the pump on the porch of the bunkhouse and put on the clean shirts they had in their saddle-bags. Their other shirts were almost immediately taken from them by a Mexican laundress, and were now clean and hanging from a clothesline to dry.

They were met at the front door by the man who had stood alongside Westbury when he accosted them at rifle point earlier.

"You're Barton?" Will asked.

"Burton, sir," the man corrected. He too had an accent.

"You're English too, aren't you?" Gid asked.

"Yes, sir."

"Are you kin?"

"I beg your pardon, sir?"

"Are you part of the family?"

"Oh, heavens no, sir. I'm in the service."

"The service?"

"It's like being part of the family," Victoria said, arriving at that moment. "Mr. Burton has worked for my father for many years, and Mr. Burton's father worked for my grandfather. In fact, the relationship goes back for four generations. Men who hold such positions refer to themselves as being 'in the service,' and it is a very old and very honorable profession."

When Will saw Victoria, he couldn't hold back a gasp of surprise. He would be hard-pressed to identify this as the same young woman he first saw yesterday. That woman had been a naked waif, a poor, bedraggled creature who was only barely managing to cling to humanity.

The woman who greeted them now looked as if she had stepped down from a fine oil painting. She was wearing an off-the-shoulder dress with a neckline that plunged low enough to show the top of her breasts, though a red silk rose, strategically placed at the cleavage, helped preserve some modesty. The dress itself was clinging, yellow silk, overlaid with lace. Her coiffure featured a pile of curls on top, and a French roll which hung down her neck. A gold chain was around her neck, and from the chain dangled a large pearl.

Will had never seen anyone quite like this before. It was as if he were being confronted by a queen or a princess come to life.

Victoria grew uneasy with the expressions on the faces of Will and Gid, and, with a nervous laugh, she touched her hair.

"Have I gone green?" she asked.

"What?"

"You are both staring with such intensity," she said.

"Oh, I'm ... I'm sorry," Will apologized. "It's just that you look so ... I mean, I've never seen..." He paused, then continued, changing his line of thought. "Uh, that is, I had no idea lunch would be such a dressy affair. I'm afraid these shirts are all we have."

"If you wish, madam, I believe I could find some jackets for them," Burton suggested. "Though, for the larger gentleman, it might be quite ill-fitting."

"Never mind, Mr. Burton, they are fine just as they are," Victoria said.

"To be sure," Burton said, looking at the two brothers with ill-concealed disapproval. "This way, gentlemen."

"That's all right, Mr. Burton, I'll take them to the dining room," Victoria said. Smiling at the two brothers, she stepped between them and offered each of them an arm.

They walked down a long, wide hall, with a floor that was so highly polished it reflected the items of furniture standing on it as clearly as if it were a mirror. Along the way, as if standing guard, were several polished suits of armor and painted shields. All the shields were decorated with the same crest. Against a white background, a blue mailed fist clutched a golden sword, placed at the intersection of a red St. Andrew's cross.

"That's the same thing that's on the door of the coach," Gid said, pointing to one of the shields.

"That's the coat of arms of the Earldom of Ravenscourt," Victoria said. "I am told, by the way, that a distant ancestor of mine, the first Earl of Ravenscourt, wore this very suit of armor in the Battle of Agincourt," she added, pointing to one of the iron suits.

"Ha! Gid, I'd hate to see you try and get into something

like that," Will said. "You wouldn't even be able to get your arm inside it."

"Was this here fella a full-grown man at the time?" Gid asked.

Victoria laughed. "Oh, yes. But the Battle of Agincourt happened over four hundred years ago, and I believe people were smaller then."

"Four hundred years?" Will gasped. "You can keep track of your kin that long?"

"That is an important date in our family, for that was when Geoffrey Westbury was invested with the Earldom of Ravenscourt," Victoria explained.

"What is this earldom?" Gid asked.

"English peers come in several degrees of importance," Victoria explained. "At the top of the order are dukes, followed by marquesses, then earls, then viscounts, then barons. My father is ... or was, an earl."

"Victoria, all that is of no concern here," Robin Westbury said, meeting them in the doorway of the dining room at that moment. "I'm sure our guests are not interested in our quaint customs."

Westbury was wearing a white uniform of some sort, with a red sash running diagonally across his chest, gold-fringed epaulets on his shoulders, and a splash of medals on his breast.

"I think it's very interesting," Will said. "I've read about kings and lords and knights and so forth, but I've never met anyone like that before now."

"Yes, well, technically, dear boy, you haven't met one now," Westbury said. "As Victoria told you, it was necessary for me to give up the title, and my land, when I left England to come to the United States."

"Did it bother you to give it up?"

"Not at all. I firmly believe that your founding fathers were quite right to dispense with titles. They are oppressive to the common man and burdensome to the peerage. But enough of that. If you'll come this way, gentlemen, I believe lunch is ready."

Westbury led them into the dining room. The dining room was a very large room with polished oak wainscoting running halfway up the walls, and flocked cream and green wallpaper finishing it off. At strategic spots around the room large portraits hung by wires from the picture rail. One of the portraits was of Robin Westbury astride a horse, wearing the same uniform he was wearing now. Another was of a beautiful woman. For a moment, Will thought it was a portrait of Victoria. Upon a closer examination, however, he realized that the young girl standing beside the woman *was* Victoria.

"That was my mother," Victoria said, noticing where Will was looking. "She died the year before we left England."

"She was a very beautiful lady."

"Yes, she was," Westbury agreed.

"I see that you are wearing the same sort of clothes in that painting that you are now," Will said. "Is that a military uniform of some kind?"

"Yes," Westbury said. "I still hold a brigadier's commission in the Royal Reserves, though I seriously doubt that the Queen will ever call me to active duty."

"My father fought in the Crimean War," Victoria said. "He was at Balaclava as a lieutenant in the Light Brigade. You may have heard of the famous poem written by Tennyson: 'Theirs not to make reply, Theirs not to reason why ...' "

" 'Theirs but to do and die,' " Will continued, taking over the poem. " 'Into the Valley of Death rode the six hundred.' Yes, I have heard of it."

"I'm very impressed," Victoria said.

"I was always impressed by the bravery of those soldiers," Will said. "It's an honor to actually meet one of them."

"I was young and imprudent. It was a foolish battle in a war fought with honor but no sense," Westbury said. "Of the six hundred troops we committed to the charge, four hundred were killed. But then, I needn't tell you gentlemen such things. Your country, and my daughter tells me that you, personally, have come through your own war with battles just as foolish, and just as deadly. Suppose we change the subject?"

Westbury pointed to the center of the dining room where there was a very long table, covered with a damask tablecloth and set with crystal candelabra, silver chargers, and glistening china. "Won't you be seated?" he invited.

The meal was brought to the table in various courses. Will didn't think he had ever tasted anything as good, and Gid obviously concurred, for his appetite and acceptance of "seconds" was so prodigious that, before the end of the meal, a few of the kitchen staff sneaked unobtrusively to the door to get a look at the man who could eat so much.

After the meal Westbury invited Will and Gid into his library. Here, twenty-foot-tall bookshelves lined the walls, and books filled the shelves. Westbury gestured toward a cluster of leather chairs, and they all sat down. There, Westbury gave them the reward he had promised. In addition, brandy was served and Victoria offered them cigars. When the offer was accepted, she trimmed the ends and ran her tongue down the length of each side. Then she lit each of them.

"Gentlemen, if you think I am plying you with food, drink, and tobacco for a specific reason, you are right," Westbury said. "I want you in a good mood when I attempt to make my case."

"Make your case?" Gid asked. He took the cigar out of

his mouth and examined the burning tip. He had never had one this good. "What case is that?"

"I want you two men to come to work for me."

Will shook his head no. "We appreciate the job offer, Mr. Westbury," he said. "We really do. But I'm afraid you wouldn't be getting your money's worth out of us. Neither one of us is a cowhand."

Westbury studied them for a moment over the rim of his brandy snifter.

"Who said anything about making you into cow-hands?" he asked.

Will looked confused. "Then I don't understand. If you don't intend to make us into cowhands, what do you want with us?"

"I want to hire you for the skill you have already demonstrated. When you killed those men who took my daughter, you proved yourselves to be quite skilled with your weapons."

"You want to hire our guns, you mean?" Will replied.

"In a manner of speaking, yes."

Will shook his head. "We aren't hired killers."

"Are you trying to tell me you have scruples, Mr. Crockett? Scruples from men who rode with Quantrill?"

Will stood up quickly, and when he did so, Gid stood up as well.

"Mr. Westbury, I thank you for the great meal, the

good brandy, and the fine cigars. But I think my brother and I will be going on now."

"No, wait... please ... wait," Westbury called, holding out his hand. He paused for a moment, pinching the bridge of his nose as if trying to gather his thoughts. "I'm sorry, the remark about a lack of scruples was quite boorish, and I beg your forgiveness. It's just that I find myself in a country that is rough and unforgiving, a country for which my experience has left me totally unprepared. Witness the scheme to abduct my daughter for ransom. If you two had not happened along at the right moment, it might have resulted in an unthinkable disaster. Luckily, you spoiled their scheme."

"We spoiled their scheme all right," Will said. "In fact, you could say we spoiled it permanently."

Westbury waved his hand. "I know, I know, you killed them all, and good riddance. I wish I could say that with their demise all danger had passed, but in the atmosphere of lawlessness that prevails, who is to say some others won't conceive of the same plan? And, of course, there are also rustlers to contend with. You said that you were not hired killers, Mr. Crockett. Well, that is good, for I have no wish to employ killers. I do, however, want to hire people who might be able to provide a measure of safety for my daughter and me, and might, at the same time, deter the lawless elements from their adventures."

"Aren't you afraid that you might be jumping from the frying pan into the fire?" Will asked.

"Are you suggesting that I might be putting myself in danger by hiring you?" Westbury asked.

"You are in no danger from us, Mr. Westbury. But you were right when you accused us of riding for Quantrill. We did a lot of robbing, burning, and killing. We aren't choirboys, Mr. Westbury. You might say we are outlaws, who had wanted posters out in several states. Are you willing to hire outlaws?"

"I am willing to hire men of honor," Westbury said. "And though you claim to be outlaws, and I've no reason to dispute that claim, you have also proven to me that you are men of honor."

"Please, Will, Gid," Victoria said. "I know, after all you have done for me, that I have no right to ask for anything more … but we need you."

"You have five thousand dollars as a reward for rescuing my daughter. I will double that, if you will stay for one month," Westbury said.

"Five thousand dollars for one month's work?" Gid asked. He whistled. "Lord almighty, that kind of pay could make an honest man of me right quick. Will, I say we stay. And if you don't want to, I'll stay by myself."

Will sighed, then chuckled. "All right, we'll stay."

Chapter Four

In the nearby town of Loraine, people were going about their business on the main street when a stranger rode in. He pulled up near the Cattle Call Saloon, dismounted, and tied his horse to the hitch rail. The townspeople watched him with increasing curiosity as he took off his hat and rubbed a handkerchief across his face. That was when they saw that he had only one half of his upper lip.

The stranger was wearing a gun strapped low on his right hip. He looked up and down the street, then, not appearing to take notice of two men who were standing on the porch of the building next door to the Cattle Call, he went inside.

"You know who that is?" one of the men asked after the man was through the swinging doors and out of hearing.

"I ain't never seen him before," the other answered. "But I've heard him described. That's gotta be—"

"Jude Sampson," the first one interrupted, as though he didn't want to be cheated out of saying it. "They say he's faster'n greased lightnin' with that gun of his. They say he's gunned down more'n ten men in fair fights."

"I was goin' to say that," the other replied. "I know'd who it was the moment I seen him. I didn't need you to tell me."

"Well, I'll just bet you don't know what he's doin' here," the first one said.

"No, I don't. But if he's lookin' for anyone, I sure wouldn't want to be that person."

"He's come to work for Dan Berriman, out at the Double-Diamond."

"That feller's come to work at the Double-Diamond? Ha! He sure don't seem like no cowpuncher to me."

"I don't figure he's goin' to be punchin' any cows."

"Then what is he goin' to be doin'?"

"If you ask me, he'll be doin' what he's been doin'. Killin'," the first answered matter-of-factly.

Inside the saloon, Sampson stepped up to the bar, and the bartender hurried over to see what he wanted. At the opposite end of the bar a couple of cowboys flanked a young woman. They were talking and laughing, and pouring drinks from the bottle of whiskey that sat in front of them.

"Whiskey," Sampson ordered.

"Yes, sir, Mr. Sampson," the bartender answered nervously. He took a glass from under the counter and, with shaking hands, poured Sampson a drink.

"You know where the Double-Diamond is?" Sampson asked.

"Yes, sir, I do. It's about five miles northwest of here," the bartender replied.

"Hey, mister," one of the two cowboys at the end of the bar called. "You goin' to work on the Double-Diamond?"

Sampson looked toward the cowboy, but he didn't answer.

"The reason I ask is, me an' ole Slim here, we punch cows for Wilbur Caswell. He owns the Cripple C, right next to the Double-Diamond. That makes us neighbors. Ain't that right, Slim?"

"That's right, Dudley," Slim answered.

Slim and Dudley were both in their mid-twenties. They were typical-looking working cowboys, wearing their prized Stetsons, vests, and leather chaps. Both were wearing pistols, though the guns were worn high and strapped in for ease of riding and working.

"You goin' to be cookin' for Berriman?" Dudley asked. "Reason I asked is, you don't much look like a cowboy, if you'll excuse me for sayin' so."

Sampson raised his glass to his deformed lips and stared at Dudley, Slim, and the woman with them. He said nothing.

"Course... they ain't nothin' wrong with bein' a cook," Dudley went on. Sampson's cold, expressionless stare was beginning to make him nervous.

"Honey, quit talkin' to him," the woman whispered. "He scares me."

"Now, how can that little fella scare you?" Dudley replied. "Hell, look at him. Skinned and gutted, he wouldn't dress out any more'n one fifteen, maybe one twenty pounds."

Sampson turned back toward the bar. "I want a woman," he said to the bartender.

"I, uh, am sorry, sir," the bartender replied. "But we have no women available."

"I'll take that one," Sampson said, pointing to the woman with the two cowboys.

"It is my belief that the two young men with her have engaged her for the entire afternoon."

"They ain't doin' nothin' but talkin' to her," Sampson said.

"Yes, sir, but once they pay their money, it is their prerogative how they spend their time."

"You," Sampson said to the woman. "Come on, we're goin' upstairs."

"What?" the woman replied.

"You heard me. I said we're goin' upstairs."

"Mister, maybe you didn't notice," Dudley said. "But Hattie's with me and my pard."

"You ain't doin' nothin' but talkin' to her," Sampson said. "When I'm finished with her, I'll send her back down."

Dudley looked at the bartender. "Tell you what," he said. "Our no lip friend there is new here, so maybe he don't understand the word 'manners.' That bein' the case, I won't go down there and kick the shit out of 'im."

"Dudley, no!" the bartender hissed, sliding down the bar quickly toward him. "Don't you know who that is?"

"No."

"His name is Sampson. Jude Sampson," the bartender said, as if the name would explain everything.

"Still don't mean nothin' to me," Dudley said. "Except that he may be just about the ugliest sumbitch I've ever seen."

"Please," the bartender pleaded. "Don't make him mad."

"Don't make him mad? Why don't you tell that little pissant not to make *me* mad?"

"Dudley, I don't have a good feelin' about this," Slim whispered. Then, more loudly, to the bartender he added, "Bartender, why don't you pour our new neighbor another drink, on us?"

"Yes, I'll be happy to," the bartender said, smiling broadly in an attempt to defuse the situation.

"I don't want another drink. I want the woman,"

Sampson said. He started down toward them and raised his hand. Dudley stepped in front of him.

"Mister, I've had about as much as I'm goin' to take from you. You touch that woman and I'm goin' to knock you on your ass," he said menacingly.

Sampson grunted with contempt, stepped around the cowboy's outstretched hand, and put his hand on Hattie's shoulder. Hattie whimpered in fear, and before Sampson's hand closed, Dudley hit him.

Sampson's reputation as a killer had, long ago, precluded even the biggest men from actually challenging him. As a result, he was taken completely by surprise, and he caught the punch on his jaw, then went to the floor like a sack of potatoes.

Dudley laughed. "I told you what I was goin' to do," he said apologetically. He reached down to help Sampson up. "Now, why don't you just leave us and the woman alone? Drink the drink my pard and I bought you, and forget it."

Sampson smoothed his clothes, then glared at Dudley.

"Pull your gun, mister," he said.

"What?"

"I said, pull your gun. Or give me the woman."

"The woman ain't goin' with you."

"Dudley," Hattie said in a frightened voice. "Dudley, I'll go with him. It ain't worth gettin' killed for."

"Hell no, you ain't goin' with him," Dudley said. "Mister, the bartender here tells me your name is Sampson, like that's s'posed to mean somethin' to me. Well, let me tell you somethin', it don't mean shit to me. Now, if you're wantin' to put up your fists and fight like a man, I aim to oblige you."

"Don't be a fool, Dudley," the bartender said. "Sampson may be the fastest man with a gun there ever was."

"Fast with a gun? That don't mean nothin' to me," Dudley said. "I ain't plannin' on fightin' him with a gun." He doubled up his fist. "All I aim to do is bruise the little shit up some."

"I'm goin' to kill you, cowboy," Sampson said, his voice cold, flat, and totally without expression.

"Told you, I ain't goin' to get in no gunfight with you," Dudley said.

"Come on, Dudley," Slim said. "This here is makin' me nervous. Let's get on back to the ranch."

"And leave this pretty girl here, all alone?'"

"Go on, Dudley," Hattie said, her voice rising in panic. "I mean it. I ain't goin' to stay with you."

Dudley looked at Sampson again, then he sighed. "All right, mister, this is your lucky day," he finally said. "Looks like I ain't goin' to beat the shit out of you after all. Come on, Slim, let's go. I reckon we can come back when the company's a little better."

"You won't reach your horse alive," Sampson warned.

"Why not? You goin' to shoot me in the back?"

"Could be."

"To hell with you, mister," Dudley said. "Come on, Slim, let's go."

Dudley and Slim started toward the door. The two men who had watched Sampson arrive, and who had been peering over the batwing doors from outside to see what was going on, now stepped to one side to let Dudley and Slim come through. Sampson followed them.

"You ain't goin' nowhere, mister," Sampson said.

On the porch now, Dudley turned to face Sampson. In addition to the two men who were already there, a few others, made curious by the scene being played out on the boardwalk in front of the Cattle Call, began drifting over to watch.

"I'm riding out of here," Dudley said again. The gravity of his situation had finally sunk in, and the bravado was gone ... replaced by a nervous tick in his voice.

"I'll make it easy on you," Sampson said. "I'm going to count to three. You can pull your gun any time you want, but you'd better do it before I get to three 'cause that's when I'm pulling mine."

"I... I don't want to do this," Dudley said. Now his voice reflected naked fear.

"You ain't got no choice," Sampson said. "One ..."

"Slim?" Dudley called.

"You ... you goin' to take us both on, mister?" Slim asked, holding his hand out over his pistol.

"Two."

Dudley made a desperate grab for his pistol. Sampson smiled at him and waited for Dudley to clear leather before he started for his own gun. Slim hesitated a second, then he began his draw as well.

For just a moment, Dudley and Slim had the irrational idea that they might just win, and wild smiles began to spread across their faces. Then Sampson's shoulder jumped and a pistol appeared in his hand, already blazing. The first shot caught Dudley in the chest, and he stumbled back off the porch, pulling the trigger of his own gun as he did so, sending a slug into the boards. Sampson's second shot hit Slim between the eyes, and he fell backward, his arms flopped out uselessly beside him. He didn't even get off a shot.

"My God! Did you see that?"

"He didn't even start to draw till them two boys already had their guns out 'n still he beat 'em!"

"Sweet Jesus, I ain't never seen nothin' like that!"

Sampson stood there for a moment, the gun still smoking in his hand as he looked down at the bodies of the two men he had just killed. Then he looked out at the men who had gathered to watch.

"Anyone here thinkin' maybe this wasn't a fair fight?" Sampson asked.

"Not me," someone replied.

"They drawed first," another said.

"It was a fair fight. Yes, sir, fair and square," another voice added.

"Good," Sampson said, holstering his gun. "Thought you might see it my way."

Several in the crowd walked over to get a closer look at the two dead cowboys. Dudley's feet, covered by well-worn boots, were turned out at an unusual angle. Slim's feet, covered with fine snakeskin boots, were pointing straight up. Slim's eyes were still open. Dudley's eyes were shut.

"Get 'em out of here," the bartender growled. "Can't leave them out like that. It's bad for business."

"What do you want to do with 'em?"

"Drag 'em over to the corner of the building there and cover 'em with a tarp till the undertaker gets here," the bartender suggested.

Sampson, with an indifferent shrug, pushed his way back through the batwing doors. Hattie was cowering in the corner of the saloon.

"You ... you killed those men," she said.

"No, I didn't. You killed them," Sampson replied.

"What do you mean, I killed them?"

"You shoulda gone upstairs with me when I asked you the first time. Now, see how foolish it was for you to say no to me? Your friends are both dead, and you're goin' upstairs with me, just like I wanted. Kind of funny when you think about it, ain't it?" he added, laughing cruelly.

Chapter Five

At Camelot, approximately ten miles distant from Loraine and Jude Sampson, Will and Gid Crockett were just outside the bunkhouse when nearly a dozen men rode in. The cowboys were tired and worn-looking, as if they had ridden long and hard. They rode straight to the watering troughs, dismounted, and began removing their saddles as the horses drank thirstily. Some of the men stuck their heads down into the same troughs, or filled their hats which they then put on, letting the water cascade down across their faces.

At first the cowboys were shouting and laughing back and forth to each other in such an animated and self-contained way that no one noticed Will and Gid. In fact, the first sign anyone had that there were strangers in their midst was when someone saw Victoria's horse in the corral.

"Hey, lookie there," one of the cowboys said as he turned his own mount loose. "Ain't that the horse Miss Westbury was ridin' when she was took?"

"I believe it was," one of the others said. "She must be back."

"Unless the horse come back on its own."

"The horse didn't come back on his own. Miss Westbury is back," Will said as he and Gid walked out to join the men who had just returned.

Surprised to see a couple of strangers amidst them, the cowboys turned toward them in curiosity. Then the one who appeared to be the leader came over to meet them. He was a short, bandy-legged man with a scar on his cheek that looked like a purple lightning flash.

"The name is Ford, Johnston Ford, though most folks just call me Choctaw," he said. "How do you know Miss Westbury is back?"

"Because my brother and I brought her back," Will said.

"You the sons of bitches that took her?" one of the other cowboys asked menacingly.

"Easy, Percy, easy," Choctaw said, holding out his hand. "If they're the ones that took her, I don't think they'd be hanging around here right now."

"You're a smart man," Will said.

Choctaw smiled, though the scar on his cheek had obviously severed the muscles on one side of his mouth because the smile pulled his lips out of shape. "Yeah, well, maybe that's why Mr. Westbury made me the foreman," he said. "We been lookin' ever'where for Miss Westbury. The boss must've been real pleased to see you two boys bring her in. Are you looking for work?"

"We already have work," Will said.

"Mr. Westbury hired us," Gid explained easily.

"Is that a fact?" Choctaw asked. He lay his finger alongside his scar and rubbed it thoughtfully for a moment.

"That's right," Will said.

"All right, what's done is done, I reckon," he finally said. He pointed a short, crooked finger at Will and Gid. "But just so's you understand ... I am the ramrod around this here outfit. Mr. Westbury mighta hired you, but you'll be takin' your orders from me, just like all the other cattle hands."

"We're not cattle hands," Will said.

Choctaw looked surprised. "What do you mean, you ain't cattle hands? If you ain't, what the hell did Westbury hire you for? What do you plan on doin'?"

"Whatever Mr. Westbury wants us to do," Will answered easily.

Choctaw's eyes narrowed. It was obvious that he didn't particularly like the setup, but it was also obvious that there was nothing he could do about it.

"All right," he finally said with a snarl. "If Mr. Westbury wants to hire you, that's his business. Maybe it's his way of rewardin' you for findin' his daughter. But if you two ain't workin' for me, then you stay the hell out of my way, do you hear me? I got no time for you. Where are you bunkin' down?"

"What's wrong with the bunkhouse?" Will asked.

"The bunkhouse is for cowboys. Workin' cowboys," Choctaw added. "There's a place behind the tack room. You two can bunk in there."

"Sounds good enough to us," Will said.

"Long as there's a place at the table for us," Gid added. He took a step closer to Choctaw and looked down on him. "And I intend to see to it that there is," he added menacingly.

"Sure, there won't be no problem with you boys settin' at the table," Choctaw said.

Gid was out just after breakfast the next morning. He enjoyed working with his hands, so when he saw that the wheels of one of the wagons needed to be packed with grease, he didn't ask anyone about it. Instead, he merely went about getting the blocks in place and the wheels off, then he started packing the hubs by hand.

Will was about to help him when Westbury came out to talk to them.

"You don't have to do that kind of work," Westbury said.

"I know I don't have to," Gid said, standing up and touching the back of his hand to his forehead. He left a small smear of grease. "But it reminds me of another time ... another place. I like it."

"Then, by all means, don't let me stop you," Westbury said. Then he looked over at Will. "Will, I would appreciate it if you would come riding with me this morning. I just got some disturbing news about Gypsum River Estuary."

"Estuary?"

"You would probably call it a creek. It is the principal source of water for the entire ranch," Westbury said.

"What about it?"

"One of my riders tells me it is dry."

"Does it sometimes run dry?"

"It floods and recedes, but it is never completely dry," Westbury said. "And with the recent rain and runoff, it should be in freshet stage right now."

"I've seen beaver completely shut down a stream. We'll go take a look," Will said.

Gid stood up then, his hands covered with grease. "Let me get some of this off, and I'll go with you," he said.

"No, you go ahead and finish the job," Will suggested. "We're just going to take a look, that's all."

When they left a few minutes later, Victoria was with them. She took great pride in describing the improvements her father had made to the land.

"Gypsum River was little more than a seasonal creek when we came here," she explained. "But Father connected the low spots and diverted the bed so that water began to follow what may have been an ancient riverbed. The result is a daily water flow that has provided sufficient water, not only for our ranch, but for all the ranches below us as well."

"That must be the creek just ahead," Will said, pointing to a long line of dark green that cut through the land.

'You've a good eye about you, Mr. Crockett," Westbury said. "That is it, indeed."

When they reached the line of vegetation a few minutes later, Will saw that they were looking down on a channel that, while obviously much larger, had dwindled down to a tiny stream of water no more than a few inches wide and a few inches deep.

"My word!" Westbury said, getting down from his horse and walking up to the edge of what had been the creek. "Look at this."

"Let's go upstream and see if we can find out what happened," Will suggested.

The three riders followed the dry streambed along its meandering course for better than five miles. Then, on the other side of a thick-growing patch of trees, they saw a large dam.

"What in the world?" Westbury gasped. "When and how did that get here?"

"It's no beaver dam, that's for sure," Will said.

"Look at the size of it, Father. It had to take whoever built it some time to do it. Why didn't we know about it?"

"We have no stock on this part of the range," Westbury replied. "And no reason to be here. Like as not they got the entire dam built, then closed the floodgates. We never realized it until the water flow stopped."

"Is that on your property?" Will asked.

"Actually, that is not," Westbury admitted. "My property line ends there, with the edge of that copse. From there on, it becomes part of Dan Berriman's ranch, the Double-Diamond. But the water the dam has captured should be flowing on my property, and thus I consider it an invasion of my estate."

Westbury, Will, and Victoria crossed over the property line, then rode up to the dam and dismounted. A man, dressed in a business suit, walked over toward them. He was accompanied by two men, one a big man carrying a rifle, and another much smaller, but because of his pale skin, his clear eyes, and the almost demonic expression on his face caused by a half lip, seemed much more dangerous-looking.

"You are trespassing on government property," the man said.

"Government property? I thought this was Double-Diamond land. Who the devil are you, anyway?" Westbury demanded.

"The name is Condon, Harris Condon," the man replied. He pointed to the larger of the two armed men with him. "This is Mr. O'Leary, one of my assistants. The other gentleman is Mr. Sampson, actually an employee of the Double-Diamond. Mr. Berriman has graciously agreed to provide one of his own people to guard the government's interest here."

"What government?" Westbury asked.

"Why, the U.S. Government, of course. I am one of their agents. And you are correct in assuming that this is Double-Diamond land, but the government has a lease arrangement with Mr. Berriman, which allowed us to build this dam."

"Yes, well, that is the crux of the whole matter, isn't it?" Westbury sputtered in anger. "Why in heaven's name did you dam up Gypsum River?"

"We did it for the public good," Condon answered.

"And what public good is coming from this?" Westbury asked.

"Water improvement," Condon said.

"Improvement? Why, you bloody rascal, you have squeezed dry every drop of water from my ranch! And not only my ranch, but those ranches below me who are also dependent upon the Gypsum as a source of water."

"While I agree that it might appear that way, Mr. Westbury, in fact what we have done here is all for the common good," Condon said. Condon took a folded piece of paper from his inside jacket pocket. "I'm glad you came here today. It will allow me to serve you with this assessment for fifteen thousand dollars."

"Assessment for fifteen thousand dollars?" Westbury asked, frowning as he took the paper from Condon. "What the bloody hell are you talking about?"

"You and all the other ranchers are being assessed to pay for the water improvement work we have done," Condon said.

Westbury read the paper, then began to cough and sputter so that Will was afraid, for a moment, that he might be suffering from some sort of an attack.

"Have you gone mad?" Westbury bellowed. "First you steal my water, and then, to add insult to injury, you tell me that I must pay for the privilege. Why, that is an outrage! I have no intention of paying this assessment!"

"I'm afraid you have no choice, Westbury. You will either pay it, or we'll confiscate your land and cattle, and sell it for the monies due us. That is the law."

"You'll do no such thing," Westbury said. "In fact, if you don't tear this dam down, I will!"

Westbury shoved Condon aside and started toward

the dam, but before he had taken three steps, O'Leary hit the Englishman with his rifle, not a skull-smashing blow, but a short, vicious chop, hard enough to drop Westbury like a sack of potatoes.

"Father!" Victoria shouted, going quickly to him.

"You son of a bitch!" Will swore. He took a step toward O'Leary, but Sampson already had his own gun in his hand, cocked.

"You take one more step, mister, and you're a dead man," Sampson said. Knowing that the ugly little maggot of a man meant what he said, Will stopped.

"You could have killed him!" Victoria said from her kneeling position by her father.

"Yes, we could have, but we didn't," Condon said. "And now, if you know what's good for you, you'll get your father on his feet and out of here. As I told you, you are trespassing on government property."

Westbury, who had gone out for just a moment, came to with a groan.

"Are you all right, Mr. Westbury?" Will asked.

"Yes, I think so," Westbury replied, rubbing the back of his head. When he brought his hand around to look at it, there was blood on his fingers.

"Mr. Westbury, you must accept my apology," Condon offered. "It is not the policy of the U.S. Government to assault people. But it is the policy to protect its property, and my deputy thought you intended to harm the dam."

"I do intend to harm it," Westbury said. "And I will bring it down, whatever it takes."

"I'm sorry to hear you reacting that way, Mr. Westbury," Condon said. "Because, of course, we can't allow that. And I'm afraid we must insist upon your paying your just assessment. You have thirty days, Mr. Westbury. Thirty days, or we will take further action against you."

"I'll be back," Westbury promised.

"If you do come back, Westbury, might I suggest you get a pass from the district office in Loraine? Otherwise, you will be trespassing and you could get shot."

Chapter Six

By the time Will, Victoria, and Westbury returned to the ranch, Westbury had grown nauseous and dizzy from the effects of the blow to his head. He was so unsteady in his saddle that for the last few miles Will had to lead his horse so Westbury could hang on. When they stopped in front of the house, Will dismounted quickly and helped Westbury from his saddle. Burton, seeing what was going on, came out quickly to offer a hand.

"What is wrong with His Lordship?" Burton asked.

"He's been hit in the head," Will said.

"Oh, my. Sir, would you help me get him to his room?"

"Yes, of course," Will said.

"Don't make such a fuss," Westbury mumbled. "I'll be all right."

Westbury took a few steps, then collapsed. Burton and Will picked him up and, as an anxious Victoria hurried alongside, carried him into the house.

"I don't understand," she said. "He didn't seem this badly hurt at first."

"I've seen it before," Will said. "People will take a blow to the head and at first seem all right. Then the wound begins to swell. I don't know, it must put pressure on the brain or something, because it gets worse."

"Could it be ... fatal?" Victoria asked anxiously.

"Sometimes it is," Will admitted. When he saw the anxiousness on her face turn to fear, he added, "Although most of the time it isn't. And your father's wound doesn't seem that bad. Probably all he needs is a day or two to rest up."

A few minutes later, after Westbury was in bed and under the watchful care of his two faithful servants, Will started asking Victoria some questions.

"Your father said you've been having trouble with cattle rustlers, but he didn't say anything about trouble with the federal government."

Victoria shook her head. "That is what was so surprising about the incident today. Up until now, there had been no trouble with the federal government at all. All of our difficulties have been with rustlers."

"You know, I've been wanting to ask you about that as well. I realize that rustlers can be troublesome, but Camelot is a huge place, with thousands of cattle. It's hard to see how a few head of rustled cattle could cause so much trouble that your father seems actually concerned that he might lose the ranch."

"It's considerably more than a few head," Victoria said. "To date, we've lost over a thousand head."

Will whistled. "A thousand head? That's quite a job. I'm amazed anyone could steal that many cows and get away with it. I mean, how would a rustler, or a gang of rustlers, get rid of so many cows without being noticed?"

"That's the mystery none of us can understand, for we aren't the only ones suffering. All the other ranchers in the area are suffering crippling losses as well. Of course, no one else has lost as many head as we have, because we have the most to lose, except perhaps the Double-Diamond."

"The Double-Diamond. That's the ranch we visited today, isn't it? Where the dam is."

"Yes, and it is nearly as large as Camelot. Especially since Dan Berriman has been expanding his acreage by buying out the smaller ranchers. He's even offered to buy Camelot."

"Has Berriman offered a fair price?"

"Who is to say? How does one put a price on a dream?" Victoria asked.

"Yes, but surely by now your father has learned that operating a big ranch is no picnic."

"Perhaps so, but Father isn't one to give up easily. Besides, where else could he go? He has no land, no home, no title back in England. When he left, all the bridges were burned behind him. No, we are here to stay, Will, whether he makes a go of it or is completely broken."

"Your father may wind up losing the ranch, but from what I have already seen of him, I don't think he will ever be broken," Will said. He looked back toward Westbury's bedroom. "Let him sleep now," he said. "That will be the best thing for him."

Victoria reached out and put her hand on Will's, then squeezed it slightly.

"Thank you," she said.

Leaving Robin Westbury in good hands, Will went back out to the barn to join his brother. By now the wagon had been greased, a hay rake had been repaired, and a dozen other jobs attended to. Gid was just finishing straightening out some harness when Will stepped into the shadows of the machine shed.

"How is Mr. Westbury?" Gid asked.

"He'll be all right in a day or two," Will said. He looked around the shed, the interior of which was light and shadow, defined by the long, thin bars of light which slashed in through the cracks between the boards.

"You look like you've had a busy day," he said.

Gid smiled. "Yeah, I have," he said. He pointed to the

shelves and tables of the machine shed. "It's been a while since anyone straightened things up in here. Why, Pa would've had a conniption fit if we'd kept our machine shed like this."

"You miss the farm, don't you, Gid?"

Gid put his hand on the leather traces of the harness he had just straightened out. "Yeah," he said. "I'd be lying to you if I told you I didn't miss it. But..." He sighed before he went on. "I know we can't go back... even if we were granted a full pardon in Missouri... we couldn't go back."

Outside the shed they heard a couple of riders coming in. Looking through the cracks between the boards, Will saw that one of the riders was Choctaw.

"Rad, soon as you can, get on down to the breaks and join the others," Choctaw said. "And don't say nothin' 'bout what we were doin'."

"You don't really think I'm dumb enough to say somethin', do you?"

"No, just bein' cautious, that's all," Choctaw replied.

"Sure hope they're not brandin'," Rad said. "I'm tired of smellin' the stink."

"Give me the brandin' iron, I'll put it back," Choctaw offered.

Rad handed the branding iron to Choctaw, then remounted and rode away. Choctaw started toward the machine shed, carrying the iron. Before he reached the shed,

Will and Gid stepped outside. Startled, Choctaw stopped.

"Afternoon," Will said.

"What the hell?" Choctaw asked, startled by their un-expected appearance. He looked back toward Rad, who was already out of earshot. "Did you hear what we was talkin' about?" he asked.

"No, should we have?" Will replied. He had heard the admonition not to speak of what they had been doing, and he found that curious, but he didn't know what it was about.

"No, it's none of your business," Choctaw said. He pointed toward the machine shed. "What was you two doin' in there?"

"Working," Gid answered. He pointed to the shed. "Take a look for yourself. I've got everything straightened up in there."

"Who told you to do that?" Choctaw growled.

"Nobody told me. I did it on my own."

"Mister, around here you don't do nothin' unless I tell you to do it. I told you, I'm the foreman."

"It's a strange kind of foreman who doesn't appreciate someone who is willing to work without being told," Will said.

"I like to know what's going on, that's all."

"You keep up with things, do you?" Will asked.

"That's a foreman's job."

"Then you no doubt will be interested to know that Mr. Westbury should recover from his injury."

"Injury?" Choctaw asked, genuinely surprised at the news. "What injury?"

"He was hit in the head by someone claiming to be a federal guard, down by the dam on Gypsum River."

"What dam on Gypsum River? There ain't no dam on Gypsum River."

"Yes, there is. The government leased some land from the Double-Diamond just across from Camelot's property line and built a dam there. Mr. Westbury, his daughter, and I visited it this morning," Will replied. "Being the good foreman you are, I would think you would've brought it to his attention before now."

"How was I supposed to know about it? I didn't know anything about a dam."

"You have noticed that Gypsum River is dry, haven't you?"

"So what? Streams fill up and dry out all the time out here."

Will shook his head. "I've been told that Gypsum River never runs dry. And even if it did, this is the wet season. Seems to me that, as the foreman, you would've noticed it before now."

"You tryin' to tell me how to do my job?" Choctaw asked.

"I'm not tryin' to tell you how to do your job," Will answered. "I'm just doin' my job."

"And what is your job?"

"The job Mr. Westbury hired me for," Will said. "To find out who's causing trouble for him."

"Yeah, well, just be careful that while you're findin' out who's causin' trouble for him, you ain't causin' trouble for me," Choctaw said.

"I'll be glad to," Will said. Then with a wry smile he added, "Unless you're the one causing the trouble."

Choctaw glared at Will for a long moment, as if measuring his backbone. Then, determining that Will was someone who could back up what he said, Choctaw looked away.

"Why don't you let me put the brandin' iron away for you?" Gid asked, waiting until after Will had stared Choctaw down.

"Why don't you mind your own business?" Choctaw growled, jerking the iron away from him. "I'll put it away myself."

Choctaw strode angrily toward the machine shed while Gid and Will stood their ground, watching him walk away.

"Not a very likable cuss, is he?" Gid asked.

"No, I don't reckon he'll be invitin' us to share a bottle with him," Will agreed.

Gid chuckled.

Just after breakfast the next morning, Will walked down to the corral to watch the cowboys saddle their broncs and ride off by twos, threes, and sometimes larger groups, to attend to their assigned tasks.

Will had learned a lot about people over the last few years, and he wanted to look into the face of each rider as they left. If Westbury's problems were coming from within the ranks of his own employees, an expression or a look might provide Will with a clue.

His experiment bore no fruit, however, and when the last rider had left, Will rejoined Gid, who had been engaged in the same task, though from a different part of the corral.

"Did you see or hear anything suspicious?'" Will asked.

"No," Gid said. "Just seemed like a bunch of guys goin' to work is all."

"Yeah," Will agreed. "Either none of them is involved, or the ones who are, are damned good at keepin' secrets."

At that moment a buckboard turned off the road and came up the long drive. There were two people in the buck-board, an older man and a very attractive young woman.

The woman was driving, and she pulled the team to a halt.

"Lordy, will you look at that?" Gid said, looking at the

woman with obvious appreciation. "You ever see anyone any prettier than that woman?'"

Will chuckled. "She's a looker, all right," he said. "I'll go see who she is and what she wants."

Gid cleared his throat. "Maybe I'd better go with you," he suggested.

The two brothers walked over to the buckboard, touching their hats in greeting as they approached.

"Howdy," Gid said, smiling broadly at the woman. Even though she was sitting down, he could see that she was tall. Her long red hair cascaded down across her shoulders, and her blue-green eyes looked out from above high cheekbones. She returned Gid's smile.

"You must be new here," she said. "I don't believe I've seen you before."

"I'm Gid Crockett. This is my brother, Will. We just started here a couple of days ago."

"I'm Mollie Vitters. This is my uncle Frank," the girl replied. "We're Mr. Westbury's neighbors, and we just learned that he was hurt yesterday. How is he?"

"You'll have to ask my brother that," Gid said. "He was with him when it happened."

"It could've been worse," Will said. "But he's much better this morning."

"Thank God for that," Mollie said.

"Is it true?" the man with her asked. "Has the damn

fool federal government dammed up Gypsum River?"

"Yes, sir, they have," Will said.

"What could they possibly have been thinking to do that?"

Will stroked his chin. "Your place must be downstream from Camelot," he said. "I take it the dam is going to be as bad for you as it is for Mr. Westbury."

"Not just as bad, Mr. Crockett," Mollie said. "It will be much worse. Camelot has a few other sources of water. The Flying V has only a few tanks here and there, and they will dry up when the summer is at its height. I don't know what we'll do then."

Victoria, having seen Mollie and her uncle arrive, came out of the house to meet them. After warm greetings, the three went back into the house.

"I don't know about you, Big Brother, but in my mind, that is one good-lookin' woman," Gid said.

"She sure is. And I'm even getting used to her accent."

"Accent? What accent?"

"Her English accent."

"Who the hell is talking about Miss Westbury? I'm talking about Mollie Vitters."

Chapter Seven

Three days later, when Westbury was fully recovered, he called a meeting of all the ranchers whose land was affected by the "water improvements." Will, Gid, and the cowboys who weren't out on the range watched the ranchers, big and small, arriving for the meeting in various means of conveyances: buckboards, democrat wagons, open stages, phaetons, country wagons, traps, and, of course, horses. Vehicles and livestock filled the curved driveway as the ranchers went into the house and gathered in Westbury's large parlor. By now, all knew about the dam and most had been assessed payment by the government. Though Westbury's 15,000 dollars was the highest amount, the others, less affluent, were proportionately just as badly hurt.

"Wilbur, I was real sorry to hear about Dudley and Slim," Homer Cyrus, another rancher, said.

"Dudley and Slim?" Westbury repeated. "Aren't they the two young men who used to work for me?"

"Yes," Wilbur Caswell said.

Westbury chuckled. "What did they do? Get a bit rowdy in town and wind up in the lockup?"

"They got themselves killed."

Westbury was surprised by the answer. "Killed? My word! How did that happen?"

"They were goaded into a fight in the Cattle Call Saloon in town," Wilbur explained. "And they were shot down."

"Heavens, I hope the authorities have the murderer under arrest."

Wilbur sighed. "According to the witnesses, it wasn't murder, it was a fair fight. Though how you can call a gunfight between two working cowboys like Dudley and Slim and a paid killer like Sampson fair, I'll never know."

"Did you say the fellow who shot them was named Sampson?"

"Yes. Jude Sampson, the infamous gunman. I'm sure you've heard of him."

"No, I've never heard of him. But I have met him," Westbury said.

"You met him?" Caswell asked.

"Yes. Ugly looking chap he is, half of his top lip is gone."

"No lip, yeah, that's him, all right. They say it got bit off by some whore, 'n when he killed her, they say it was justifiable homicide on account of what she done."

"What was he doing out at the dam?" Frank Vitters asked.

"I think he was providing some sort of guard duty. I was told that he is in the employ of Dan Berriman."

"Let me get this straight. He's workin' for Dan Berriman, but he was standin' guard over a government dam?"

"Yes, that appeared to be the case," Westbury replied.

"Boys, if we needed any proof that Berriman was behind all this, that should be it," Wilbur said.

"Yeah, well, Berriman ain't hurtin' none, that's for sure. Fact is, he's still buyin' land from those who will sell to him," one of the owners said.

"That's true," Homer Cyrus agreed. "He's made me an offer for my land." He paused for a moment before he went on. "And I have to tell you boys, I think I'm goin' to take him up on it."

"What did he offer you, Homer?" Westbury asked.

"He's offered to buy my stock at ninety percent of the market price, give me two and a half dollars an acre for my land, and he'll pay the assessment charges himself."

"Two and a half dollars an acre?" Westbury scoffed. "Why, Homer your land's worth twenty times that and you know it."

"It's worth that with water," Homer agreed. "But without water, that dirt ain't doin' nothin' but holdin' the world together. Hell, if it wasn't for the fact that Berriman has been lettin' my cows onto his rangeland for water, they'd all be dyin'."

"You mean Berriman is letting your stock water on his range?" someone asked.

"Yeah," Homer answered. Then he added, "But he's takin' every third cow for payment."

"Every third cow? My God, that's what he's askin'?" Frank Vitters exclaimed. He shook his head. "And here I was, thinking about going to him, hat in hand, to see if I could work out a deal. But, every third cow?"

"Tell me, Mr. Vitters, you do agree that keeping two thirds of your herd is better than letting all of your cows die of thirst, don't you?" a new voice suddenly asked. "And when you consider that I have a rather large herd of my own to look after ... perhaps you'll realize that my offer is fair."

Westbury and his guests looked toward the door of the parlor. What they saw standing there was a man who had no hair of any kind, no eyebrows, and no eyelashes. Even his chin was as smooth-skinned as a woman's.

"Yeah, well, what is it costing you, Berriman?" Wilbur Caswell asked with a growl. "You got more water now than ever before. Hell, we all know that you're the only one who benefited from this Yankee government water project."

"That's true, I have benefited," Dan Berriman admitted easily. He looked at Westbury. "Robin, I know that I wasn't invited to this meeting, but I hope my presence isn't unwelcome. If it is, I shall move on without delay."

"Of course you are welcome here, Dan," Westbury said graciously. "I hope you don't consider your omission a slight. It's just that since you aren't facing the same water problem the rest of us are, I thought you wouldn't be interested."

"Nonsense," Berriman said. "If my good friends and neighbors are hurt, then so am I. I want us to find some way to resolve this problem, if we can."

"Do you have any suggestions, Mr. Berriman?" one of the other ranchers asked.

"Yeah," another put in. "Can you tell us how to get our water back?"

"I'm afraid I have no answer to that problem, gentlemen," Berriman replied. "Although I did discuss this very matter with Mr. Condon at some length. I even asked him if he would remove the dam, or at least install a sluice to allow a measured amount of water through. But he turned me down. Apparently the government is quite committed to improving the water system for this part of the country."

"Improving the water system?" Westbury said. "You know, I do believe that is the most disturbing aspect of this entire bizarre affair. How could anyone possibly call this dam an improvement?"

Berriman removed a pipe from his jacket pocket and began stuffing the bowl with tobacco.

"Well, Robin," he said calmly, all the while tamping down the tobacco, "I can see why such a thing might get you riled. But we have to take a look at the long-range view of this operation. When I spoke with Mr. Condon, he told me that if the water system isn't improved, the time will come when this whole basin will be as dry as a desert. Now, we certainly don't want that, do we?" -

"Hell, the Yankee sons of bitches are turning it into a desert now!" one of the ranchers protested angrily.

"Be that as it may, gentlemen, it *is* a government project and, as such, we are not able to get it changed. But my offer still stands to all who would want to take advantage of it. You may lease water rights from me in exchange for one third of your cattle."

"That brings us back to where we were when you came in," Westbury said. "Isn't that rather steep?"

"If you don't want to do that, you can sell your land to me," Berriman suggested.

"At two dollars and fifty cents an acre?" one of the ranchers asked.

"It's a fair price, under the circumstances," Berriman insisted.

"You already know my answer, Mr. Berriman," Homer Cyrus said. "I am accepting your offer."

"Yes, Homer, and I appreciate your vote of confidence," Berriman replied.

"Homer, won't you reconsider?" Westbury asked.

Homer shook his head. "Look, I know when I'm licked. If I don't sell at two and a half per acre now, I'll be lucky to get twenty-five cents an acre for it by the end of summer. I really don't have any choice."

"What about you, Robin?" Berriman asked.

"I'm not interested in selling my land," Westbury said.

"I know. I was speaking about my offer to water your herd."

"For one third?"

"That's my price."

"You are asking me to turn over at the very least eight thousand cows to you. At twenty-five dollars a head that's two hundred thousand dollars, just for water rights!"

"Yes, it is," Berriman replied easily.

"Well, I won't do it," Westbury insisted. "I can't do it!"

"I'm sorry you feel that way," Berriman said. "For a thirst-maddened herd the size of yours could be quite dangerous."

"We haven't reached that point yet," Westbury said. "Although Gypsum River is my primary source of water supply, I do have some other sources."

"You're talking about Bird Creek?"

"Yes, I'm talking about Bird Creek."

"Well, Bird Creek is running now," Berriman said. "But it will be bone-dry by the end of August, and then you will be in the same boat as everyone else. What will you do then?"

"We have a saying for that in my country," Westbury said. "Perhaps you have heard it. 'That bridge shall be negotiated when it is reached.'"

"Robin, I hate to say this," one of the other ranchers said. "But Berriman is right. If we don't make some sort of agreement with him, we stand to lose everything."

"We've got to do something," another said.

"All right, but not this," Westbury pleaded. "Don't sell out everything that you have worked for."

"Have you got any better ideas?"

"I don't know yet, but I'm thinking about it," Westbury said. "And I will come up with something."

"That's fine for you, Mr. Westbury, you are a wealthy man and you can afford the loss. Plus you have Bird Creek. I know that ain't much water, but if it wasn't for a few tanks left over from the rain, we wouldn't have no water at all."

"I'll share my water with you," Westbury offered.

"Robin, you can't do that, you barely have enough for your own stock," Vitters said.

Westbury waved his hand as if dismissing Frank's precaution. "It doesn't matter," he said. "We are all in this together. We'll find a solution together... or we'll go down together."

The other ranchers applauded.

"Very commendable, Robin," Berriman said. "And I wish you well. Oh, before I leave, I would like to remind you gentlemen that I am hosting a barbecue for all the working cowboys in the area, at my ranch tomorrow. It's my way of expressing appreciation to them for the thankless job they do for all of us. And whether you, personally, are prepared to do any business with me or not, I do hope you will at least allow your hired hands to attend."

"I've only got four hands left," Frank said. "But I think they're plannin' on being there."

"Same goes for my boys," another said.

"Two of mine won't be there," Wilbur Caswell said dryly. "Them bein' Slim Eaton and Dudley Stone."

"Yes, I know about those two," Berriman said. "They should've known better than to try and brace a professional gunman, but you know how it is with young men like that ... they get a few drinks in them, and it is my understanding they were showing off in front of a prostitute who worked in the saloon. Still, it is regrettable and I expressed my feelings about it to Sampson. He has assured me that he will go out of his way to avoid any such confrontations in the future."

"Yes, I'm sure he'll be as meek as a Sunday school teacher," Wilbur growled.

"Gentlemen, I seem to have disturbed the equanimity of your gathering. If you will excuse me, I'll take my leave now."

"You mark my words," Wilbur said after Berriman was gone. "Somehow that son of a bitch got the government to build that dam. I don't know how he did it, but he did it as sure as a gun is iron."

The meeting broke up shortly after Berriman left, and, though nothing concrete had been resolved, Westbury's offer to share his diminishing water supply with those who already had none gave the ranchers a little more hope and resolve. Even Homer Cyrus suggested that he might not sell out after all but would stick it out for a little longer. Then, in twos and threes, the vehicles and horses started back down the long, curved driveway, the first step of the journey back to their own places.

Frank Vitters and his niece Mollie accepted Westbury's invitation to stay for supper and beyond, and, shortly after the last visitor left, Burton came out to the tack room. The tack room, or rather the small room behind it, was where Will and Gid were making their quarters. If Choctaw thought he was making it uncomfortable for

Will and Gid by banning them from the bunkhouse, he was mistaken. For several years now, the two brothers had made their home wherever they might find it, under the shelter of an overhanging rock, in a cave, or a bedroll under the stars. With its two beds, table and chairs, and kerosene lantern, the tack house was pure luxury compared to their normal quarters.

Will was sitting at the table, using the lantern light to read a book he had borrowed from Westbury's library. Gid was sitting on the edge of his bed, carving on a forked stick, when Burton knocked on the open door, then stuck his head in.

"I beg your pardon, gentlemen," Burton said in his low-pitched, cultured voice.

"Yes, Burton, what is it?" Will asked.

"Lord Westbury is extending an invitation for the two of you to join him and Miss Westbury and their guests, the Vitters, for dinner."

"Mollie Vitters?" Gid asked quickly, looking up from his carving.

"I believe that is the young lady's name," Burton replied.

"Hell yes, we'll come!" Gid said excitedly, without waiting for confirmation from Will. "Tell them we'll be there!"

"Very good, sir," Burton said as he withdrew.

Gid put down his forked stick and began going through his roll. Then, with a triumphant snort, he pulled out a pair of trousers.

"There they are," he said. "I knew I had a clean pair."

"Clean pants and a clean shirt? What's bringing on this sudden display of vanity, as if I didn't know?" Will teased.

"It doesn't hurt to look good ever' now an' then," Gid said. "Listen, you remember that bottle of bay rum I bought back in Austin? Have you seen it anywhere?"

"You used it all up as a mosquito repellent, didn't you?"

"That's right," Gid said. "Damn me for a fool. I shoulda saved some of it."

Will chuckled. "Well, hell, Little Brother, if it'll ward off mosquitoes, what makes you think it won't ward off Miss Vitters?"

"Yeah," Gid agreed. "Yeah, maybe you got a point there." He felt his rough chin. "Well, the least I can do is shave."

Half an hour later both brothers, washed and freshly shaved, wearing clean shirts and clean trousers, though without the benefit of any bay rum, once again found themselves at the dinner table in Westbury's posh dining room. Gid, by his own manipulation, was sitting next to Mollie. Will was next to Victoria. Robin Westbury and Frank Vitters were sitting at opposite ends of the table.

"I could trim my herd, I suppose," Westbury said. "Cut it back by about a third. That would make the water go a bit farther."

"What about when the water dries up?" Frank asked.

"Yes, well, it's only completely dry for about a month and a half," Westbury replied.

"You think any cow on this range is going to survive forty-five days without water?"

"Probably not, but I don't have any idea what else to do."

"Why don't you dig some wells?" Gid asked easily. He pointed to the platter of biscuits.

Westbury looked at Gid as if he were answering the suggestion of a child.

"Wells would be wonderful, of course," he said. "But, where to dig them?"

"Would you mind if I had another three or four of the biscuits? They're really good."

"My, you do have an appetite, Mr. Crockett," Mollie said, reaching for the platter.

"Yes'm, I reckon I do," Gid admitted. "Mr. Westbury, if there is a natural supply of water aboveground, then there's water underground."

"Yes, an aquifer," Westbury said. "I am quite familiar with the concept. Still, the question remains, where do you dig? You can't just go out there and dig a hole any-where and hope to find water. And even if you did, how would you get it out of the ground?"

"Getting it out of the ground is easy," Will replied. "All you have to do is put in some windmills."

"Windmills? Good heavens, you mean like those huge monstrosities one finds in Holland?"

"Holland?" Gid asked, putting butter on one of his biscuits. "Don't think I've ever been there. That's up north, somewhere?"

"Holland is a country, over in Europe," Will explained. "No, Mr. Westbury, I've seen pictures of the windmills they have in Holland. I'm not talking about anything like that. The windmills we would use are quite small compared to those. They are little more than wooden frames, with mounted blades. The blades spin in the wind, and in turning operate a pump. The pump will bring up the water and fill whatever sized tank you want to dig. If you have enough of those placed about your ranch, then it won't matter if you never get Gypsum River back. And if you set the example, I'm sure all the other ranchers would do the same thing."

"Yes, that would be wonderful," Westbury agreed. "But you haven't answered the most important question. How will we find the water?"

"Oh, you don't have to worry about that," Gid said, taking half the biscuit with one bite. He chewed thoughtfully. "I'll find it for you."

Mollie laughed. "You'll find it?" she asked.

"Yep."

"And just how do you propose to do that?" Westbury asked.

"By dowsing for it," Gid answered. "I've already cut myself a dowsing stick. It's a good one too."

"A dowsing stick?" Westbury asked, his face a mask of confusion. "What in the blazes is a dowsing stick?"

"Some folks call 'em divining rods. I used them all the time back in Missouri, before the war. We had three wells on the family farm, and I found all three of 'em."

"He also found wells on several other farms," Will added. "My brother's the best dowser I ever saw. Don't worry about where the water is, Mr. Westbury. Gid'll find it for you."

"I appreciate the offer," Westbury said dismissively. "But I would not like to put my faith in witchcraft."

"This isn't witchcraft," Gid said, the expression on his face showing that he was hurt by the accusation. "It's a science."

"Father, I think we should let him try it," Victoria said. "After all, what do we have to lose?"

"She's got you there, Robin," Frank agreed. "All in the world can happen is the boy will either find water or he won't. If he does find it, it could be the solution to our problem. And if he doesn't find it, well, then we are no worse off than we are now."

Westbury was silent for a moment, then his face broke into a big grin. "Of course you are right," he said. "We won't lose anything by trying. All right, Mr. Crockett, I accept your kind offer. When would you like to start this scientific experiment?"

"How about tomorrow?"

"Tomorrow it is."

"Wait," Victoria said. "What about the barbecue Mr. Berriman is giving for all the cowboys tomorrow?"

"What barbecue?" Gid asked.

"Berriman was just here," Westbury explained. "Evidently, he is hosting some sort of appreciation for the working class tomorrow. He has invited all the hands from all the neighboring ranches to attend something he calls a barbecue."

"And having observed your appetite firsthand," Victoria said, smiling, "I'm sure you wouldn't want to miss out on the opportunity to have a grand meal."

"I know," Mollie said. "If you would want to stay here and dowse, we could have our own picnic. That is, if it's all right with you, Victoria," she added quickly.

"Why, I think that would be a wonderful idea," Victoria answered. "A dowsing and a picnic. Who could ask for a more entertaining day?"

Chapter Eight

The next morning Gid Crockett was the center of attention as he started out across a meadow, carrying his dowsing stick in front of him. Will, Westbury, Victoria, Mollie, and Frank were walking behind him. Choctaw and a scattering of cowboys were behind them, all looking on in fascination as Gid walked in a zigzag pattern across the meadow.

"What's he doin'?" one of the cowboys asked.

"He's lookin' for water."

"With that stick? How's he goin' to find water with a stick?"

"He ain't."

"I don't know, I seen it done oncet," a cowboy named Percy said.

"You getting any sign, Gid?" Will asked after half an hour of dowsing.

"Not so much as a twitch," Gid replied. He lowered the forked stick, then pulled out a handkerchief to wipe the sweat from his brow.

"Maybe there's no water on the place," Will suggested.

"No, there's water here," Gid said.

"How do you know?" Choctaw asked.

"Because I can feel it," Gid replied.

Choctaw snorted a scoffing laugh. "Boys, we ain't ever goin' to be thirsty again," he said sarcastically. "The big fella here is goin' to find us all the water we need with that there stick."

Several of the cowboys laughed.

"I think we should give him the opportunity to prove his experiment, Mr. Ford," Westbury said. "He just started."

"Yes, sir, well, me an' Rad has got some work to do, anyway," Choctaw replied. "We can't hang aroun' here all day."

"You want me and some of the other boys to come with you, Choctaw?" Percy asked.

"No, Percy, Rad and I can handle it just fine," Choctaw answered.

Percy cleared his throat then and looked around at his friends who, by the expressions on their faces, the nods, grimaces, winks, and jerks, were urging him to go on.

Percy cleared his throat again. "Uh, listen, Choctaw,

then seein' as you don't need us, is it okay if me and several of the boys go on over to that barbecue they're a' havin' at the Double-Diamond?"

"Yeah, it's all right with me if it's all right with the boss," Choctaw replied, looking toward Westbury.

"No doubt Berriman will use that opportunity to make an effort to hire you away from Camelot."

"He can make all the effort he wants. It ain't goin' to work with me, boss. I like it here," Percy said.

Westbury chuckled. "Very well, boys, if you gentlemen believe you can stand up to whatever enticement he may offer, then by all means, go and enjoy yourselves."

"Thanks, boss," Percy said, smiling broadly. "Come on, boys. They say they's goin' to be some women there."

Amidst a chorus of thank-you's and general expressions of appreciation and anticipation, the cowboys who had gathered to watch the dowsing now headed en masse toward the corral.

"Mr. Ford, are you sure you and Rad wouldn't like to go as well?" Westbury offered. "I'm sure that whatever you have to do can be put off a day."

"Nah, we can't go. If we don't get it done today it'll just be that much more work when we do get around to it," Choctaw answered. "I reckon we'd better see to it."

"I admire your discipline," Westbury said. "And I appreciate your dedication to duty. Lord knows what kind of trouble we would be in around here if you weren't foreman."

"Well, sir, I believe in a day's work for a day's pay," Choctaw said. "Come on, Rad. We have work to do."

The other cowboys, by now saddled and whooping and laughing at each other over their anticipated day off, rode out, heading toward the Double-Diamond. Shortly after that Will saw Rad go into the toolshed and come out with a branding iron. Then he and Choctaw left as well, heading in the opposite direction.

"Robin, much as I'd like to watch this, I have to be getting back to my own place," Frank said. "My own boys will, no doubt, be over at the Double-Diamond, and I think someone should be there to watch over things."

"Yes, well, I've got some papers to take care of myself," Westbury said. "And it is getting a little warm out here. Mr. Crockett, how long do you think it will be before you have some results?"

Gid lowered the divining rod. "Well, now, I couldn't tell you, Mr. Westbury. Sometimes the thing just about jumps out of my hand, sometimes you don't get anything more'n a twitch or two. So far today I have nothin' at all. I plan to keep on looking though."

"I appreciate that," Westbury said. "But you understand, you're under no obligation to find water. That wasn't part of our agreement."

"I know it wasn't," Gid said. "But if there's water here, and I believe there is, then I plan to find it for you."

"You haven't forgotten, have you, Mr. Vitters, that we are going to have our own picnic here?" Victoria asked.

"You young people go on and have it without me," Frank invited. "Mollie, you'll find a way home?"

"Yes, Uncle Frank," Mollie replied. "I'm sure Mr. Crockett would escort me." She looked directly at Gid as she spoke.

"Yes, sir, I'd be very pleased to take your niece home," Gid said, quick to take advantage of the opportunity that had just presented itself. He had no idea that Victoria and Mollie had already "divided the spoils" this morning, each laying out her claim for the Crockett she would go after.

"Well, then, it's all settled," Mollie said. "Unless you have some objection," she added, looking toward her uncle.

Frank held up his hand and chuckled. "You two ladies seem to have planned this like some military operation," he said. "I wouldn't think of raising an objection."

Chapter Nine

It took an hour of steady riding before Choctaw and Rad reached their destination, an arroyo which Westbury and all the others on the ranch believed was a dead-end canyon. It wasn't dead-end at all, but had a deceptive aperture which, though hard to find, provided a way for horse, rider, and even cattle, if carefully driven, to pass through the arroyo then emerge into a hidden valley on the other side.

The pass was a narrow chasm, masked by a high-standing needle rock. It was a ragged vent in the walls of red stone. The first five hundred feet was difficult enough going that it discouraged all but the most hardy, then it opened into a wide, flat field some twenty or so acres in size. Water was not natural to the canyon, but the recent damming of Gypsum River had diverted a stream here that was wide enough and deep enough to supply the needs of almost a thousand head.

There was grass too, though not enough to last very long. There was just enough grass to sustain the cattle until the re-branding had been completed and they were taken out the other side.

There were half a dozen cowboys camping near the assembled herd, and they came over to greet Choctaw and Rad as they arrived.

"If you'd leave that brandin' iron here, we could move a lot faster," one of them suggested.

"Not on your life," Choctaw growled. "My deal with Berriman is that I get five dollars for every head I turn over to him with the Double-Diamond brand. And the only way I can keep an accurate count is if I brand 'em myself."

"Are you sayin' we ain't honest? You think we might cheat you?"

Choctaw snorted. "Hell, Foster, you're a damn cow thief. How dishonest can you get? Yes, I'm sayin' you might cheat me. Now come on, let's get started."

"We got a hundred or so head penned up over there, ready to start," Foster said.

Choctaw took the *W* branding iron with him and went over to lay it in the fire. A moment later, when the *W* at the end of the iron was gleaming red, he nodded, and one of the cows was brought over to him and held. Choctaw picked up the branding iron and, inverting the red-hot *W* above the branded *W* which was already on the cow's hide, stuck the iron against the cow's flesh. The cow bawled and jumped, and the smell of smoke and burned animal flesh assailed the nostrils.

When Choctaw pulled the branding iron away, the two opposing W's had become two diamonds. The cow, which a moment earlier had sported the *W* brand of Camelot, was now clearly wearing the identity of a cow belonging to Dan Berriman's Double-Diamond spread.

"There you go, fellas," Choctaw said. "That's another five dollars Berriman owes me."

Rad laughed. "Just think, in no more'n thirty seconds, you earned enough money to take one of Annielee's girls upstairs with you for a whole night."

"That'll sure be a change for you, Rad," one of the rustlers said. "Most of the time you work a whole night to be able to take one of Annielee's girls upstairs with you for thirty seconds."

Choctaw and the rustlers laughed.

"You want to know somethin' curious, Gid?" Will asked. Will and his brother were alone in the meadow, still walking back and forth across it, waiting for the divining rod to make its mysterious dip.

"What's that?"

"Well, I'm the first to admit that I don't know much

about ranchin', but it's curious to me that Choctaw and Rad would have so much branding to do at this time of the year. Seems to me like the only time they'd be doing any serious branding is right after calving."

"Yeah," Gid said. "Well, it can't be all that serious or he'd have taken some more men with him. Must just be a few mavericks here and there."

"I suppose you're right. Still, it makes you wonder why he's willin' to do it himself instead of givin' the job to someone else."

"Well, don't forget the barbecue. Maybe he's just a nice guy and he figured to do the work himself so the other boys could go over to the Double-Diamond."

Will laughed. "Choctaw a nice guy? Yeah, and pigs can fly."

As promised, when noon came around, Victoria and Mollie came out to the meadow to join them, bringing a picnic lunch in a hamper. They came without Westbury, not because he wasn't asked, but because he was smart enough to get the broad hint that his company really wasn't expected ... or wanted. The two women spread a cloth out on the ground, then opened the basket to display a couple of fried chickens, a pan of freshly baked biscuits, baked beans, coleslaw, and an apple pie.

Victoria was relatively quiet during the meal. That too was by design, for she and Mollie had agreed that Mollie would use this opportunity to "get better acquainted with Gid." Thus, during the discussion they learned that Mollie's father had been killed during the war. As her mother had died many years before that, she had no place to go except to Frank Vitters, who was her father's brother.

"He sounds like a good uncle," Gid said.

"Oh, he's been a wonderful uncle," Mollie said. "But he's much more than an uncle. He's like my mother and father as well."

At that very moment Frank was pulling into the front yard of his own ranch, his team lathered from the exertion of an all-out gallop for the last two miles. The dramatic entrance was because Frank had seen smoke climbing into the sky from a couple of miles back, and though he prayed hard that it be something else ... he knew that it had to be his house. That fear was quickly borne out by the flames, which were licking high into the sky from a house that was now little more than fuel for the blazing inferno.

A short distance from the burning house, Frank saw a few saddled horses tied to a tree, and he jumped down from the wagon and ran toward them. There were two men standing near the horses, and he was shocked to see that one of them was Dan Berriman.

"Berriman, what are you doing?" Frank shouted. "Why

are you just standing there, watching? Why aren't you trying to put it out!"

"Put it out? Now, why would we want to put it out, Mr. Vitters, when I am the one who started it?"

"What? Are you telling me you're the cause of this? Why? For God's sake, Berriman! Why would you do such a thing?"

Dan Berriman rubbed his hand across his bald head.

"It didn't have to be this way," he said. "You could've sold out to me."

"You ... you bastard!" Frank said. "That's why you had your damned barbecue! You wanted to get my men away from here!"

"You're a smart man, Mr. Vitters. Isn't he a smart man, Sampson?"

Sampson! Frank looked around and saw a third man, one he had not seen earlier. He was small and bestially ugly, exactly fitting the description of the killer he had heard the others talking about at the meeting yesterday.

"You—you are the one who killed Wilbur's two men," Frank said.

"You're right, Mr. Berriman. He is a smart man," Sampson said.

"Get off the Flying V, you sorry bastard," Vitters ordered. He looked over at Berriman and the others. "All of you! Get off my property now."

"I'm afraid we can't do that," Berriman said. "You see, you came back too early."

"What?"

"If you had come back later and found your house already burned, you might have sold out to me. But now that you know I am the one who burned it... well, you can understand, can't you? I'm afraid this changes everything."

Suddenly Frank realized what Berriman was saying. Berriman was telling him that he was about to die.

Frank's anger was replaced by a cold, gripping fear. He made an urgent grab for his pistol, but Sampson had been watching and waiting for this precise moment. With an evil smile Sampson pulled his pistol and had it out and leveled at Frank before Frank could even clear his holster. Seeing that he was beaten, Frank stopped in mid-draw and started to put his gun back. "All right, you win," he said.

"Uh-uh, it don't work that way," Sampson said. He pulled the trigger, the gun roared, and a finger of flame stabbed toward Frank.

Frank felt a heavy blow to his chest, then a numbness, then nothing.

"What do you want to do with him?" the other man with Berriman and Sampson asked.

"We'll take him over behind the barn and leave him there," Berriman suggested.

"Hey, boss, if this guy is dead, how will you ever get this land signed over to you?" the man wanted to know. He had to struggle alone under the weight of Frank's body, for neither Berriman nor Sampson offered to help.

"The ranch will now pass on to his niece," Berriman said. "And I'm quite sure she won't be so stubborn."

For Gid and Mollie it had been a pleasant, almost leisurely ride back to the Flying V from Camelot. But when they crested the last hill and saw the blackened, still smoldering timbers of what had been the house, Gid had a sudden flashback to a similar scene he had witnessed some years earlier, shortly after the outbreak of the war.

At the war's beginning, neither he nor Will had made a commitment to either side. Their family didn't own slaves, and they had never owned slaves, so they couldn't see putting their lives on the line to protect the rights of those who did.

On the other hand, they weren't interested in fighting for a federal government against their friends and neighbors. As a result they had managed, for the better part of a year, to stay out of the war.

But that had all changed on the day they returned home from a four-day business trip they had taken on behalf of the family farm.

They had seen smoke rising from the vicinity of their

farm, but it hadn't concerned them.

"Pa must've just burned the brush. I can still see a little wisp of smoke up there," Will commented. "I thought he was going to wait for us."

"Probably just wanted to show us up," Gid replied. "You know Pa still swears that he can outwork the two of us together."

Will chuckled. "Yeah, well, the hell of it is, I think he can."

They reached the crest of the hill and looked down toward where the house, barn, and other outbuildings should have been. But there were no buildings there. Instead there were several blackened piles of burned-out rubble, all that remained of what had once been the barn, smokehouse, outhouse, and house. Two lonely brick chimneys marked each end of what had been the house and, from the charred skeletal remains, wisps of smoke still curled up into the bright blue sky.

"Gid!" Will shouted. He slapped his heels against the sides of his horse and it broke quickly into a gallop. Gid did the same with his horse, and they covered the last hundred yards in just a few seconds.

"Ma! Pa!" Will yelled, leaping from his saddle and looking around. Gid was right behind him.

"How'd they let the place catch on fire?" Gid asked.

"It didn't catch on fire," Will answered. "This fire was set."

Gid had that same sick feeling now that he had had then. And he had the same certainty that this fire had been set.

"My God! What happened?" Mollie asked in a thin, anxious voice. "Our place! It's burned down! Uncle Frank!" she shouted. "Uncle Frank!"

Mollie slapped her legs against the sides of the horse she had borrowed from Camelot, urging it into an immediate gallop.

Gid, because he had a bad feeling about what Mollie might find, put his horse to gallop as well, trying to head her off. "Mollie! No, wait!" he called to her.

Mollie was a good horsewoman, well mounted, and considerably lighter than Gid. As a result she reached the ruins of the house several seconds before Gid did, and she was already dismounted and looking through the burned-out rubble by the time Gid arrived.

"Oh, my, look at this, Gid," she moaned. "Look at it. It's gone, all of it." Mollie ran her hand through her hair in despair. "I can't imagine how this could've happened." She looked around, her face contorted and on the verge of tears. "And where is Uncle Frank? We have to find him. I must go to him. He needs me now. This ... this house was his entire life!"

"You wait here," Gid suggested. "I'll look around for him." But seeing that the team Frank had driven was still standing in harness in front of the buckboard, Gid feared the worst.

"No, I'll go with you," Mollie said. She shuddered. "And please, don't say no, I don't think I could stand to be left alone right now."

Gid nodded, then reached out and put his hand on hers.

"All right," he finally said. "You can come with me. We'll have a look around."

They found Frank Vitters a few minutes later, lying in a crumpled heap behind the barn where he had been left. Mollie began to cry, but she had been prepared for the worst and so finding him this way was not as much of a shock as it could have been.

"Is there anything I can do for you?" Gid asked. He felt helpless before her sorrow, but he understood it well because he and his brother had found their parents murdered in the ruins of their home.

"Gid, would you put him on the buckboard and take him into town for me, please?" she asked. "He was a vestryman in the church, and I think he would like to be buried in the churchyard." She looked back toward the burned house, then began crying again. "Though I have no idea what he will be buried in. He doesn't even have a suit, now that everything has been burned."

Chapter Ten

Mollie needn't have worried about what her Uncle Frank would be buried in. He was buried wearing one of the finest suits in Robin Westbury's wardrobe. Westbury had insisted upon it, just as Victoria had insisted that Mollie wear one of her own dresses. With all of her things destroyed by the fire, and with no place to go, Mollie had no choice but to accept the Westburys' generosity, and she did so in the same graciousness with which it was offered. She was taken into their household and treated as if she were a member of the family.

Frank Vitters had been a longtime resident of the valley and was very well liked by all who knew him. As a result the funeral, which was held in Grace Episcopal Church, was attended by all the neighboring ranchers, large and small, as well as by the businessmen of the town. So large was the crowd that the entire service had to be held outside, in the cemetery, in order to accommodate all of the mourners.

The cemetery was typical of all the other graveyards Will had seen. It covered about an acre of land, a cluster of tablets, crosses, and obelisks in wood and stone. Flowers decorated many of the graves. Here and there, small Confederate flags hung limp in the still air while the tombstones by which they stood would proudly proclaim the deceased's service in the "Ninth Texas Cavalry," or "Capp's Company," or "Hardesty's Brigade," ghost units, commanded by specters, in a phantom army.

Will and Gid were standing several yards away from where the burial was taking place. They were under a grove of cottonwood trees, near a large tombstone which had been erected over the grave of a departed Confederate colonel who was one of the specter commanders of that phantom army. They were standing with several of the cowboys, not only from Vitters's ranch and Camelot, but from the neighboring ranches as well. The cowboys were easily separated from the ranchers and businessmen, not only because they were in clean shirts and denim trousers, as opposed to the suits and ties of the ranchers and businessmen, but also because they were men who were obviously uncomfortable in large crowds. They were present for the funeral, but in choosing to stand apart from everyone else they were sharing their private world only with others of their own kind.

Vitters had four hands working for him when he was killed and all four were present for the funeral, not only saddened by the loss of their boss, whom they truly liked, but also anxious as to what their own future would hold now that Frank Vitters was gone. Would the Flying V continue? Would they have jobs?

"You're the one who found Mr. Vitters, aren't you?" one of Vitters' hands said to Gid.

"Yes," Gid answered.

"Is it true that Miss Mollie was with you when you found him?"

"Yes."

The cowboy grunted. "Must've been hard on her," he said. "But she's a hardy woman with lots of grit. I reckon she'll get over it, all right." The cowboy stuck out his hand. "My name is Arnold. I been workin' for Mr. Vitters ever since I got back from the war."

Gid introduced himself and his brother.

"You didn't see anything unusual around the ranch before it happened, did you, Arnold?" Will asked.

Arnold shook his head. "Didn't see a thing a'tall. Of course, me an' the other boys was over to the Double-Diamond at the barbecue they was havin'."

"Yeah, we know about the barbecue," Gid said. "That's why Mr. Vitters went back home when he did, because he thought someone should be lookin' after the ranch."

"Damn, I'm real sorry to hear that," Arnold said. "That makes me feel kinda responsible."

"Why? You had no way of knowing anything like this was going to happen."

"No, I guess not. But I can't help feelin' that way, none-theless. I started not to go, you know. I wish now that I hadn't. Maybe if I'da been there, the two of us could'a run the rustlers off."

"You think that's who it was? Rustlers?" Will asked.

"Well, yeah, it would have to be rustlers, don't you think?" Arnold asked. "I mean, from what I hear, they've been workin' the area pretty good. Near 'bout ever'one has lost some cattle to them. The wonder is that Mr. Vitters is the first one to get hisself kilt."

"He ain't the first," one of the other cowboys said. "What about them two boys got themselves kilt in the Cattle Call couple of weeks ago?"

"That was different," Arnold said. "They wasn't kilt by rustlers. They was kilt by that feller that only has one lip."

"That would be the one they call Sampson?" Will asked.

"Yeah, Sampson. That's him, over there, by that wagon. You heard of 'im?"

"No, not till we got here," Will answered. "Some of the boys out at Camelot were talking about him, and about how he shot down a couple of the Cripple C boys in the

Cattle Call Saloon."

"I hear tell that now, whenever Sampson goes into the Cattle Call, or any other saloon, folks give him all the room he needs," Arnold said. "He's a sawed-off runty little bastard, and if it wasn't for them guns, any normal man could break him in two. But there is them guns... and that's why Berriman hired him."

"Gid," Will suddenly said, "have you taken a good look at Berriman? Doesn't he look sort of familiar to you?"

Gid looked at Will, then shook his head. "No, I can't say as he does. Somebody looks like that, I don't think I'd forget him."

"I know it would be sort of hard to forget someone like that," Will agreed. "Still, there's something about him that's nagging at me. I just wish I could put my finger on it."

At the other side of the graveyard, Dan Berriman saw Will and Gid Crockett for the first time.

"I'll be damned," he said. "It's the Crockett brothers."

"What's that?" Sampson asked.

"Standing over there, with the group of cowboys. Do you see the two men who are apart from the others? One of them is wearing a green shirt, the other a red plaid."

"Yeah, I see 'em."

"That's Will and Gid Crockett."

"Never heard of 'em."

"You ever heard of Quantrill?"

"Quantrill? Yeah, I've heard of him. He was one of them bushwhackers, wasn't he?"

"He wasn't *one* of the bushwhackers, he was the leader of 'em," Berriman said. "And those august gentlemen rode with him. In fact, they were two of his best."

"You knew 'em, then?"

"Oh, yes, I knew them. And they knew me, but I was a different person then." Berriman ran his hand over his bald head, then pulled it down across a face that had been changed and rendered hairless by the explosion. "I was a very different person then."

"You want me to kill 'em?" Sampson asked. He asked the question as easily as if he had just inquired if Berriman wanted him to saddle a horse for him.

"I'll let you know when I want someone killed," Berriman replied.

"Whatever you say. You're the boss," Sampson said. He walked over to stand behind the wagon as the funeral continued. He watched the proceedings, or, more specifically, he watched Mollie Vitters. He had never seen the woman before today, but he liked knowing that she was the daughter of the man he had killed. That pleasure was further enhanced by the fact that he was here, at the funeral of a man he'd killed, watching the grief of that man's niece.

He would like to get her alone, and tell her that he was the one who'd killed her uncle, then he would let her know what was in store for her. He longed to see the hot flash of panic she would exhibit when she realized she was going to die.

And how will I kill you, my pretty one? Sampson asked himself, continuing to coast on the pleasurable sensations. Will I strangle you? Will you die by my knife? Will I shoot you?

In the final analysis, it didn't really matter how she died, as long as she died by his hands ... and as long as she died with foreknowledge. Her understanding, and the terror that went with that understanding, fueled Sampson's most exquisite pleasure.

The graveside remarks were concluded at that moment, and at the invitation of the rector, Mollie stepped over to the edge of the open grave and began to spill dirt down onto her uncle's coffin while the priest intoned the committal.

"For as much as it hath pleased Almighty God in His wise providence to take out of this world the soul of our deceased brother Frank, we therefore commit his body to the ground: earth to earth, ashes to ashes, dust to dust."

After the funeral Westbury asked Gid if he would drive the buckboard with Victoria and Mollie back out to the ranch. Then he asked Will if he would go with him to speak with the barrister.

"To speak to who?"

"The barrister," Westbury repeated. "A solicitor, an attorney, a lawyer," he finally explained, finding the word he was looking for. "I am going to engage him to fight against this scandalous water improvement project."

"A lawyer," Will snorted. "Sure, I'll go with you, but as far as I'm concerned, you're wasting your time."

The law offices of Seely, Hamilton, and Poole were across the street from the bank. Will and Westbury tied their horses off in front of the office, then went inside, where they were greeted by a rather smallish man in a vested suit and wire-rimmed glasses.

"Lord Westbury," the clerk greeted obsequiously. "How nice to see you."

"Hello, Bernard," Westbury returned. "Is Mr. Poole available?"

"I'll check, sir. I believe he is back from the funeral. Terrible tragedy, Mr. Vitters being killed like that."

"Yes, it was."

A moment later the clerk returned. "Mr. Poole is in his office," he said. He looked pointedly at Will. "Is this gentleman with you?"

"Yes, and he'll be going in with me," Westbury said.

"All right, Mr. Westbury, you may go in now," the clerk replied.

Douglas Poole was a large man whose girth strained against the buttons of his vest. A gold watch chain stretched across the same girth gave the appearance of being added as a way of reinforcing the overworked buttons. He greeted Westbury with an extended hand.

"Robin, my friend," he said. "How nice to see you, though, admittedly, under sad circumstances." He shook his head and made a clucking noise. "Poor Frank."

"Yes, it was terrible indeed," Westbury said. He turned to Will. "Douglas, I would like you to meet someone I have recently employed. Mr. Will Crockett."

"Crockett?" Poole said, screwing up his face. "Might I have heard that name somewhere?"

"It is possible, Mr. Poole," Will said without elaborating.

"Yes, well, what can I do for you, Robin?" Poole asked. Realizing that it was not always healthy to pursue certain subjects, he let the question of whether or not he knew Will drop.

"Douglas, are you aware of this so-called water improvement project that the federal government has started?"

"Yes, of course I am," Poole replied. "But what do you

mean, so-called? It was our office that made the application on behalf of the Valley Cattlemen's Association. Why, you yourself are a member of that organization. Don't you remember when we discussed it last year? How we wanted to follow the example you had set by what you did on your own ranch, and clean out all the channels and streambeds to provide a better distribution of water throughout the valley."

"Yes, I remember that discussion," Westbury countered. "But this has nothing to do with that. I'm talking about the dam that closed off Gypsum River, denying Camelot and every other ranch that depended upon Wolfhole as a source of water. In fact, only the Double-Diamond seems to have benefited."

"Wait a minute," Poole said, looking surprised. "You say a dam was built?"

"Yes."

Poole walked over to a table and began shuffling through papers until he found what he was looking for, a map of the valley. He spread it out on the table, holding the corners down by various makeshift paperweights.

"Now," he said. "Show me where the dam is."

"It's right here," Westbury pointed out. "It is just beyond the boundary lines for Camelot, on public land." Westbury drew his finger down Wolfhole, tracing it across his land, and also following the tributaries that ran from Gypsum River over to adjacent ranches. "And, as you can see, putting a dam here has a disastrous effect on every other piece of property around."

Poole stroked his chin. "Yes," he said. "Yes, I do see how that could have disastrous effects. I don't know what to tell you, Robin. This isn't at all what the project was intended to do. If you don't mind, I'm going to have a look into it."

Westbury smiled. "Mind? Douglas, that is exactly what I want you to do. That's why I came to you."

Chapter Eleven

Percy Wilcox, one of the cowboys at Camelot, became so intrigued with Gid's dowsing that he began following him around, watching in curiosity and offering his services when needed. For the first three days after the funeral, Gid continued to explore the grassy meadows of Camelot, without so much as a twitch from his dowsing stick.

After observing him closely for a while, Percy cleared his throat. "Say, Gid, can I try it?" he asked anxiously.

"All right," Gid answered. "But first, you'd better let me show you how it's supposed to work. Now, you see how this stick is shaped like a wishbone?" he said, holding it out toward him. "What you do is, you hold on to these two arms here. That makes the single arm stick out from the other side, so what you have is an upside-down *Y*."

"Yeah, I know, I know, I been watchin' you," Percy said. "Why don't you let me try it, Gid? I can do it. I know I can do it."

"Sure, if you want to try, go ahead," Gid said. He handed Percy the divining rod, and, almost immediately, the stick pointed down.

"No, you don't want to do that," Gid explained. "You have to keep it out straight."

"Well, I tried to," Percy said, "but soon as I held it out, it just went down by itself."

"Wait a minute, let me see that." Gid took the stick back and held it out over the ground where Percy had been holding it. As it did when it was in Percy's hands, the single arm of the inverted *Y* pointed straight down. Gid laughed.

"What is it?" Percy asked. "Did I do somethin' wrong?"

"Wrong? No, you did it right. Percy, my boy, you have the gift," Gid said. "I've been looking for water for at least three days, and you find it the first time you touch the stick."

"You mean you think there's water under the ground here?" Percy asked.

"I know there is," Gid replied.

"Well, hell, what are we waitin' for? Let's start diggin'. I'll get us a couple of shovels," Percy said excitedly as he started back toward the tool shed.

"No, we won't use shovels. There's a better way," Gid answered. "I'll show you."

By noon Will and Gid had rigged a simple water drill.

It was the same kind of drilling rig they had used to dig wells on their father's farm, back in Missouri. The drill consisted of three eight-foot poles, formed into a tripod. A pulley was at the apex of the tripod. A rope ran through the pulley, then was tied to a hollow piece of three-inch pipe which hung in perpendicular suspension just beneath the pulley. It was operated by pulling on the rope to lift the pipe, then letting the pipe fall. The weight of the fall would dig up a little of the earth. As it continued to fall, it would dig a hole, bringing in fresh dirt at the bottom of the pipe and pushing out old dirt from the top.

For a while, several people were interested enough in what was going on that the first couple of hours had no end of onlookers, kibitzers, and even a few helpers. By late afternoon, however, with no reward for their attentiveness, most had drifted away to find other tasks to keep them occupied.

Percy, alone, did not lose interest. After all, it was his dowse that had found the sign in the first place, and he was determined to see it through. The result was that, as the long afternoon shadows began to fall across the meadow, only Will, Gid, and Percy were left, sweating in the sun, pulling on the rope and letting the pipe drop, pulling on the rope and letting it drop, pulling it up and letting it drop, over and over again so that by now the hollow pipe was dropping into a narrow hole that was some twenty feet deep.

"Listen to that," Percy said after one drop.

"What?"

"I heard a gurgle," he said excitedly. "We must've hit water!"

"Drop it in again," Gid ordered, and the pipe was drawn up and dropped again. This time when it was brought up, Gid reached down to the bottom of the pipe, grabbed a handful of the detritus, then began examining it.

"What have you got, Little Brother?" Will asked.

"Mud," Gid replied with a wide grin. He opened his hand to show his find. "We'll be drinkin' water out of here before nightfall."

"Yahoo!" Percy cheered, throwing his hat into the air. "We found it! We found water!"

The cowboys who were close enough to hear the shouting came running out into the field to see what was going on. They brought others, and, when the excitement reached the house, Westbury, Victoria, and Mollie came out as well. Even Burton, still impeccably dressed in his cutaway jacket, stood by smiling happily at the scene.

" 'Pon my word," Burton said quietly. "Who would have ever believed such a thing?"

"How much water do you think there is?" Westbury asked.

"There's a lot of water down there, Mr. Westbury," Gid

said. "We can put wells in all over the place. You won't have to worry about water anymore."

"Mr. Crockett, you have my undying gratitude," Westbury said. "You are Moses in the wilderness. You have come to deliver us from the evil of the desert."

"I wish I could take all the credit, Mr. Westbury," Gid replied. "But the one you should be thanking is Percy. He actually found the water."

"You did?" Westbury asked.

"I reckon I did," Percy replied, beaming. "Gid just give me the stick an' the next thing you know, it was pointin' toward water."

"He has the gift," Gid said. "I wouldn't want to tell you how to run your ranch, but if I were you, I'd make him my full-time water finder. You're goin' to have to have someone around to take care of things after my brother and I are gone."

"Good idea. If you don't mind, Percy, I would like you to stop doing whatever else you have been doing, and help Mr. Crockett find other areas to put in the wells. That will also help you get the experience you will need later on."

"Does that mean I don't have to punch any more cows?" Percy asked. He smiled broadly. "Seein' as how cows is the dumbest critters God ever put on earth, I'd be real happy to quit messin' with 'em and go to doin' somethin' else! I'm not sure how Choctaw is goin' to take it, though."

"You have my permission to tell Mr. Ford of the new arrangement," Westbury said. "If he has any objections, tell him to come see me."

"Yes, sir," Percy said happily. "Gid, I'm goin' to go tell Choctaw, then I'll be back to start lookin' for some more wells."

Percy had come under quite a bit of teasing in the last few days for believing in Gid, and even helping him. Now he was completely vindicated as most of the others came around to shake his hand and pat him on the back, congratulating him for being the one to actually find the water.

Percy was enjoying the accolades of all his friends, but the person he had most wanted to know about his participation in finding water was Choctaw. Choctaw had made no bones about the fact that he considered the entire dowsing business to be a waste of time. Once or twice he had even intimated to Percy that if he didn't get back to his regular duties, he would be fired. Now Percy wanted Choctaw to know about his new position. He was working directly for Mr. Westbury himself now. He figured that would mean that Choctaw could no longer hold the threat of firing over his head.

But Percy was frustrated when he saw that Choctaw wasn't in the bunkhouse, corral, or tool shed. He wandered around the place looking for him, and finally wound up in the barn. Standing in the open door at the back of the barn, backlit by the bright day so that he was in silhouette, Percy saw Burt Thompson. Burt was the ranch farrier, and he was, at that moment, holding a horse's hoof between his knees, filing on the hoof. Burt looked up as Percy approached.

"Well, the hero of the hour," Burt said. He continued to file, and the file made a scraping sound.

"What do you mean?"

Burt knocked the file against a block to clear it, then blew on it before he resumed the task at hand.

"Well, didn't you find water?"

"Yes," Percy replied. "That is, I helped, but it was mostly Gid Crockett." Percy began looking back into the shadows at the rear of the barn.

"Who are you lookin' for?" Burt asked.

"Well, I was sort of lookin' around for Choctaw," Percy answered. "Ain't been able to find 'im."

Burt chuckled. "Wanna say, I told you so, huh? Well, I can't say as I blame you."

"Yeah, well, not just that. Mr. Westbury, he wants me to search for water full-time. That means I won't be workin' for Choctaw no more."

"I'm sure that breaks your heart," Burt joked.

"You seen 'im around?"

"Yeah, matter of fact, I have. He and Rad rode out of

here couple of hours ago, headed south." Using the file, Burt pointed in a southerly direction.

"Thanks," Percy said. "Think I'll ride out and look for him."

"You sure you want to do that? Like as not, he'll be back by nightfall."

"The quicker I tell him, the quicker I can get started in my new job," Percy said as he began saddling a horse. "You say you saw him and Rad headin' south? You got any idea where they was goin'?"

"No," Burt said. He scratched the side of his nose as if in heavy thought, then he smiled. "But Choctaw was ridin' the paint, the one I just shoed the other day. And the right forefoot is carrying a tie-bar shoe. You prob'ly won't have no trouble trackin' 'im down."

"Thanks," Percy said, swinging into the saddle then and heading out toward the south.

As Burt promised, the tie-bar shoe made it easy to pick up their trail, and he was able to keep his horse going at a pretty good clip.

Half an hour later Percy was totally confused. The trail had led him into a dead-end canyon and now the trail was gone. It was almost as if Choctaw and Rad had purposely swept the tracks away, as if they didn't want to be followed.

But why would they do something like that?

Percy shook his head, then raised his canteen and took a swallow of water. He recorked the canteen, then wiped his mouth with the back of his hand and looked around.

Where could Choctaw and Rad have disappeared to? The canyon was surrounded on three sides by sheer stone walls, so there was no way out, and no sign to indicate that they had turned around to leave the same way they had entered.

Shaking his head at the mystery of it, Percy hooked his canteen back onto his saddle and started to turn his horse. That was when he heard it. The faint sound of a bawling cow.

Percy stood in the stirrups and looked toward the three walls. Where did that sound come from? There was nothing in here. The walls were solid in front of him, solid to the right of him, solid to left.

He looked toward the wall at the left. Maybe it wasn't quite as solid as the other two walls. It did jut out toward the center somewhat, though he didn't see any opening.

Finally, he decided to ride up to the east wall and have a closer look.

"Damn me," he said aloud. "I believe there's an opening behind that bulge."

Urging his horse on, he rode right up to the wall. The bulge, he discovered, wasn't a bulge at all. It was, instead, a needle-shaped rock, set forward from the wall by a few feet. And behind the needle shape, there *was* an opening. It was small and could only be seen if someone was right there, and even then they had to be looking for it. But it was there, and it was big enough to allow a horse and rider to get through.

For the first one hundred yards or so Percy thought he had made a mistake coming in here. The path from the opening climbed, sometimes rather sharply, and the floor was so filled with rock that it made the footing quite treacherous.

But he rode on, driven now as much by curiosity as by any need to find Choctaw. The echoes of his horse's footfalls rolled up and down the high-walled fissure as if they were rolling timpani.

Ahead of him, and even above the sound of his horse's hoofbeats, he could hear the rattle of rock upon rock. The noise grew loud and urgent, and by the time Percy figured out what it was, he just barely managed to pull up in time to avoid the fall of several fist-size rocks. He didn't know what had caused them to fall, but from the amount of rock and stone on the ground, it was obviously a frequent occurrence.

Percy was about to turn around and go back when, once more, he heard the sound of a bawling cow. And this time there was no mistaking where it came from. It was coming from straight ahead.

Now he was nearly consumed with curiosity. Why did the hoofprints disappear? Where did this hidden trail lead to? And what was the source of the cow sounds he was hearing?

The passageway became even more narrow until Percy could reach out and touch either side. Then the path quit climbing. It continued on an even level for the better part of fifty yards, then it started going back down. And, as it went down, it widened until finally it was a broad, easily negotiated path. Then ahead, just beyond a large boulder, Percy saw an open field.

"I'll be damned," he said aloud. He slapped his legs against the sides of his horse, putting it into a canter. When he reached the flat field, he saw hundreds of cattle milling about in this, a natural corral.

What were these cows doing here? Where did they come from?

Looking around further, Percy saw that there was a branding operation in progress.

"What the hell?" Percy mused aloud. "What would they be brandin' at this time of year? Besides which, them cows is full-growed."

By now consumed with curiosity, Percy started toward the group he saw doing the branding. Most of the men were strangers to him, but he recognized Choctaw and Rad.

"Hey, you! Who are you?" one of the strange cowboys asked when he looked up and saw Percy upon them. Hearing the cowboy's exclamation of surprise, Choctaw turned around. When he saw Percy, his eyes opened wide.

"Percy, what the hell are you doing here?" Choctaw asked.

It took Percy only a moment to realize what was going on. Choctaw, Rad, and the other men weren't branding cows, they were making adjustments on a brand that had already been burned into the cows' hides. The brand that was there was the *W*. Choctaw was using another *W* branding iron, but this time he was inverting it, closing the top of the existing brand with his new brand so that the end result was two diamonds. The Double-Diamond.

"My God!" Percy said. "Choctaw, what are you doin' with these men? They're rustlin' Camelot cattle!"

Percy turned his horse around and started back toward the opening at full gallop.

"Don't let the son of a bitch get away!" Choctaw shouted, and he and the others with him pulled their guns and began blazing away.

Primer caps snapped and charges exploded as the robbers began banging away at Percy. Percy bent low over the horse's withers, urging him to go faster. A bullet carried off his hat, another whistled by his ear, and he saw still others kicking up dirt and chipping rock in front of him.

For a moment it looked as if Percy might make it. Then a bullet crashed into the back of his head and he tumbled off his horse, dead before he hit the ground.

The horse, panicked by the shooting, continued at a gallop, even faster now without its rider. With empty stirrups slapping against its flanks, it ran back through the pass, then headed toward the ranch.

"See iffen you can knock that leaner plumb offen there, Mo," one of the cowboys called.

Mo Eubanks spit in his hands and rubbed them together, then held the horseshoe in front of his eyes, sighting on the stake at the far pit.

"He's goin' to do it," one of the watching cowboys said.

"The hell he is. I'll tell you what he's goin' to do. What he's goin' to do is knock that there horseshoe right down onto the stake an' I'm goin' to have me another ringer," Burt boasted.

Burt was generally known as the best horseshoe thrower on the ranch, but a young cowboy named Mo was having a particularly good day today and was giving the champion a run for his money.

"Come on, Mo, you can do it," someone called. "I got a quarter ridin' on you!"

"Careful, Mo, careful," someone else urged.

Mo rocked back and forth, then swung his arm forward, tossing the shoe. It knocked Burt's leaner away, hooked onto the top of the stake, spun around three times, then dropped with a satisfying clang as a ringer. The toss guaranteed the win, and everyone cheered Mo, not because Burt was unpopular, but because Burt was so seldom beaten.

Burt, with a wide grin, was the first one to congratulate Mo.

"Well," he teased, "I guess I must've taught you too well."

At that very moment a saddled but riderless horse came trotting up.

"Hey, look at that," someone called.

"Where'd that horse come from?"

"Ain't that the horse Percy was ridin'?"

A couple of cowboys ran out in front of the horse and held their hands out toward the tired but still skittish animal. With shushing sounds they calmed it, then reached out and grabbed the reins.

"This is Percy's horse," one of the cowboys said. "I recognize his saddle."

"Gussy, look here," the other cowboy who had helped catch the horse said. He was standing on the opposite side.

"What?"

"Here, on the saddle. This here's blood, ain't it?"

Chapter Twelve

Mo said he thought Percy had a brother back in Arkansas, but he wasn't sure. Burt said it might have been a cousin. It wasn't until the funeral when Felix Tucker, one of the four men who had worked on the Flying V before Vitters was killed, cleared it up for them.

"Me an' Percy come out here from Mississippi together," he said. "He's got a sister back in Grenada, but they don't get along any too good. She married a Yankee carpetbagger, and Percy wouldn't have nothin' to do with him, or her either."

"Hell, who could blame him for that?" Mo said. "Ain't bad enough those Yankee bastards come down here an' take all our land, they got to take our women too."

"What are we goin' to do with Percy's things?" Burt asked.

"Mr. Tucker, you knew Percy longer than anyone

else?" Westbury asked.

"Yes, sir, I reckon I did."

"Then I shall give his saddle to you," Westbury said. "I believe that is his most valuable possession."

Felix grinned. "Why, I thank you, Mr. Westbury. That's plumb decent of you."

"The rest of you men, draw lots for what is left. That seems to be the only fair thing," Westbury continued. Neither Will nor Gid had put their names in the pot, so they were able to watch the drawing dispassionately. Choctaw, because he was the foreman, was also out of the drawing, and was standing to one side watching the proceedings. Will ambled over to talk to him.

"Mr. Westbury said you and Rad are the ones who brought Percy in," Will said.

"That's right," Choctaw replied.

"Where'd you find him?"

"Up north, near the breaks."

"You sure about that?"

Choctaw glared at Will. "Some reason I ought not to be sure?" he asked.

"No, not really, I suppose," Will said. "But his horse came in from the south."

"What the hell does that mean?" Choctaw growled. "Horses is dumb as dirt. He probably wandered around out on the range for a while until he found the place, that's all."

"Yeah, that could be," Will agreed. "Though horses usually come back home in a straight line. 'Specially if they're somewhat skittish, like that one was."

"Look, I don't know nothin' about his horse," Choctaw said. "All I know is where Rad and me found the body. It was up by the breaks."

"If you say so," Will said. "Although, it does seem a little odd that he left here heading south, and his horse came back in from the south."

"Look, I don't know what you're tryin' to make out of all this," Choctaw said. "And, anyhow, what business is it of yours?"

"None, I reckon."

"That's what I figured," Choctaw said with a dismissive snort.

"Choctaw says they found him up north," Will said to Gid that night as the two brothers discussed the situation in their little room behind the tack room.

"Yeah, I heard he was saying that," Gid said. "But Burt swears he saw Percy ridin' south to look for Choctaw."

"Yeah, and south is where Choctaw has been goin' just about every day," Will said.

"Which means the son of a bitch is lyin' when he says he found Percy up by the breaks."

"That's right," Will said.

"You think Choctaw killed Percy?" Gid asked, studying Will through hooded eyes.

"Yeah, I think he did," Will answered without hesitation.

"The only question is, why did he kill him? What would he stand to gain?" Gid asked.

"Don't forget, Choctaw and Rad have been leaving out of here every day, going south with a branding iron in their saddlebag. I think Percy happened onto them while they were doing something they shouldn't have been doing ... like perhaps changing the brands."

"You mean you think Choctaw's stealing cows? From Mr. Westbury?" Gid asked.

Will nodded. "He's stealin' cows, and my guess is, poor old Percy must've stumbled onto them. When he threatened to tell, Choctaw or Rad shot him."

"Yeah, well, whoever did it did more than just shoot him. He had half a dozen bullet holes in him," Gid said.

Gid heard someone outside, in the darkness, coming in from riding nighthawk, the horse's hoofbeats ringing hollowly. From over in the bunkhouse he heard a man's low, rumbling voice, followed by the laughter of several of the cowboys. Out on the prairie he heard a coyote howl.

Chapter Thirteen

Will was absolutely positive that Choctaw was rustling Camelot cattle. He was going to suggest as much to Westbury, but every time he mentioned Choctaw's name, Westbury would make some comment as to how lucky he was to have found a man like Choctaw to run his ranch for him. It therefore became obvious to Will that before he accused Choctaw, he was going to have to have some proof.

It was to obtain that proof that Will and Gid decided to spend a few nights out on the range just to keep an eye on things. They told no one of their plans, not Westbury, neither of the women, and none of the cowboys, since they didn't know who among the cowboys would be loyal to Choctaw and who would be loyal to the man who actually paid their wages.

Will and Gid rode out onto the range early in the afternoon, and when it grew dark, they took up a position that would enable them to keep an eye on the herd, or at least as much of the herd as the moonlight would show. They built a campfire, then let it burn down until the flickering flames were gone so that there remained only the red and orange gleam of the embers. An open can of beans sat on a flat rock Will had put inside the glowing coals, and a small wisp of steam curled from the top. Will and Gid sat near the fire waiting for the beans to warm. Will leaned over to look into the can.

"Looks like it's about ready," he said. "We'll cut up a pepper or two and it'll be a fine meal."

"It's a hell of a long way from being a meal, no matter what you do to it," Gid snarled.

"Gid, I swear, boy, you'd bitch if you were hung with a new rope," Will chortled.

Out in the darkness a calf, separated from the others by a casual shifting of the herd, bawled in fright, to be answered by the reassuring call of its equally anxious mother.

"Did you bring any peaches?" Gid asked hopefully. Both brothers had a fondness for canned peaches and, whenever they could, kept one or two tins of the fruit in their saddlebags.

"We ate the last of the peaches, remember?" Will answered. He tasted a spoonful of beans. "Oh, I love 'em," he said. "They're great."

Gid held out his tin plate, and Will spooned half the

can onto it. Gid took a mouthful, then made a face.

"You love 'em, you say? I'll tell you one thing, Big Brother, if you ever get hitched up, your wife's goin' to have an easy row to hoe to please you, 'cause if you love this, it sure won't take much."

"Hitched? Now how the hell can I ever get hitched?" Will teased. "Seems to me like I took you to raise."

Both men heard it at the same time. It was a quiet sound, a subtle sound which the average person might never have discerned, but which stood out sharply to senses which, over the war years and in the time since, had been finely honed to discern potential danger. The sound they heard was horse's hooves, as distinguished from the clatter of the hooves of thousands of milling cattle.

"Someone's comin' around," Gid hissed.

"Yeah, I hear," Will replied. Both plates of beans were set down as the men moved quickly toward their rifles.

Will made a silent motion with his hand to send Gid around one side, while he started around the other. They moved stealthily through the night, toward the sound of the intruder.

When Will reached an open area, he ran through the night, crouched low, keeping an eye on the ground before him in the dim moonlight so he wouldn't trip. Off to his right was a large mass of cattle, the herd he and Gid were watching. Beyond the herd the horizon was blocked out by the large, dark mass of a nearby mesa. That made it impossible to see in silhouette anyone who might be sneaking around.

Will followed the meandering Bird Creek up to a higher elevation. It was Bird Creek and its meager source of water that had sustained the herd since Gypsum River was dammed. Will couldn't help but notice how little water remained in Bird Creek now, which made the wells he and Gid were digging all the more important. Within a month, Bird Creek would be dry and the wells would be the only source of water. But with two wells in and a third begun, Will felt certain they would be equal to the task.

Will reached a rock outcropping about three quarters of the way up the draw, and he lay flat on it and looked out over the herd. It was difficult to see anything more than a large, black mass.

"Will!" Gid yelled. "I see two men over toward the butte!"

A flash of fire and a rifle shot followed Gid's call, and Will knew that he had fired on the men.

The rifle shot startled the two horsemen into activity and they both left at a gallop. Their sudden movement and the sound of their horses alerted Will to their presence, and he too fired at them, not really trying to hit either of them, but merely trying to spur their retreat on.

"Yaaheeeeeehah!" Gid screamed, giving the Rebel yell.

"Look at them sons of bitches skedaddle!"

Will hurried back down the creek bank until he returned to their campsite. He had gone farther than Gid, so Gid was already there by the time he returned.

"Who do you think that was?" Gid asked. He was still pumped up with the excitement of the encounter, and his smile and wide eyes told Will he was enjoying this more than digging wells. "You think it was Choctaw?"

"No, I don't think so," Will answered. "I just got a glimpse of 'em. I didn't see them clear, but neither one of them sat their saddle the way Choctaw or Rad does."

"Yeah, well, maybe it wasn't Choctaw or Rad, but I'll bet it was cattle rustlers. They probably thought that over on this side there wouldn't be anyone watchin' over the herd."

"The reason they thought that was because they were probably told that," Will said. "By Choctaw," he added.

"What was that?" someone's voice called from the night.

"Anybody see anything?" another voice asked.

"Listen, boys, we better split up and ride around the herd," another said. "Like as not, they're real skittish about now."

Will started putting out their campfire. "Gather up your gear, Gid," he hissed. "Let's move back out of the way until they get the herd quiet again. I'd just as soon not be seen out here. I don't want to answer any questions."

"Good idea," Gid agreed.

Will and Gid moved their camp far enough away from the edge of the herd to avoid being discovered by any of the night-riding cowboys, and there they spent the night. The next morning the first pink fingers of dawn touched the sagebrush, and the light was soft and the air was cool. Will liked the range best early in the morning. He liked the way the last morning star made a bright pinpoint of light over the purple range mountains which lay in a ragged line far to the west.

Will got a fire going, then threw chunks of mesquite wood onto it, stirring the fire into crackling flames which danced merrily against the bottom of the suspended coffeepot. A rustle of wind through feathers caused him to look up just in time to see a golden eagle diving on its prey. The eagle swooped back into the air carrying a tiny desert mouse which kicked fearfully in the eagle's claws. A rabbit bounded quickly into its hole, frightened by the sudden appearance of the eagle.

Will poured himself a cup of coffee and sat down to enjoy it. It was black and steaming, and he had to blow on it before he could suck it through his extended lips. He watched the sun peak above the nearby mesa, then stream brightly down onto the open range.

Gid had gone out a short time ago to take a look around. Now he came back in.

"Uhm, uhm, that coffee smells awful good," Gid said, swinging down from his saddle and walking toward the fire, rubbing his hands together in eager anticipation. "I wouldn't mind havin' a biscuit and some bacon, either."

"I've got some jerky in my saddlebag if you'd care for any," Will said.

"No, thanks," Gid replied. "I reckon I've eaten enough range candy when I had to. I'm not so hungry now that I can't wait till we get back to the cookhouse where we can get us a real breakfast."

"Can't say as I blame you," Will said.

Gid poured himself a cup of coffee, and as Will had before him, blew on it, sucking it noisily through his lips.

"Will, I saw somethin' strange out there," Gid said.

"Strange? What do you mean, strange?"

"Out there, by the washout, I found tracks goin' into the herd."

"Into the herd?"

"Yeah. It's like, instead of comin' to steal cattle, they were here to bring some back. Now, why would they do that, do you reckon?"

"Maybe it was going to be like a Judas goat," Will suggested. "You know, bring a lead steer in, have him mix with the herd, then cut away, bringing several cows with it. That's what they sometimes do in a slaughterhouse."

"Could be," Gid said. He chuckled. "Only thing is,

this cow now belongs to Camelot."

"Yeah. We probably not only saved Westbury's cows, we saved the other ranchers' cows as well. Even ole Berriman ought to thank us."

"Berriman," Gid snorted. "Hell, it wouldn't surprise me if that son of a bitch wasn't behind all of this, the way he tried to cheat all the other cattlemen out of their water."

Will tossed the final dregs of his coffee into the fire. "Well, what do you say we get on back to the ranch? If we start now we'll be back in time for breakfast, and no one will ever know we spent the night out here."

The nearest town to Camelot ranch was Loraine, Texas, and in his office in Loraine, a nervous Harris Condon examined the letter that had arrived with the morning post.

UNITED STATES DEPARTMENT
OF THE INTERIOR
WASHINGTON, D.C.
August 23, 1870
The Honorable Harris Condon Commissioner, Water Resources Loraine, Texas
Dear Mr. Condon,
This department is in receipt of a letter, dated the 3rd, instant, in which the writer, Mr. Douglas Poole, a lawyer in Loraine, Texas, raises the claim that the water improvement project in your charge has deprived several ranchers

of the water which normally flows across their land.

You are directed to visit Mr. Poole and the ranchers who have raised the claim and explain that the clearing out of canals and channels will increase, and not decrease the flow of water. You will also assure him that there are no plans for a dam, as he has expressed some concern about an alleged dam across Gypsum River.

An inspector will be in your area one month from now, and he will help you explain the project to those who are apprehensive about it.

Your Obedient Servant,

Columbus Delano Secretary of the Interior

Condon put the letter to one side, then poured himself a stiff drink. What was he going to do when the inspector arrived? There was no dam authorized, and yet the dam at Gypsum River was most obviously there.

Berriman, he thought. It was Berriman who'd persuaded him to build the dam in the first place. It was Berriman who'd convinced him that in the long run the dam was better for the ranchers because it would preserve the water. It was Berriman who had said he would guarantee that there would be no trouble as a result of building the dam, and it was Berriman who'd furnished the "deputies" who stood guard while the dam was being built, one of whom had nearly caused a catastrophe by attacking Robin Westbury. Fortunately, Westbury had survived and there were no repercussions ... but if the blow had been a little more severe, the result could have been disastrous.

The situation was becoming untenable and Condon was going to have to find some way out. And, as far as he was concerned, the person to show him the way out would have to be Dan Berriman.

Condon had sent for Berriman as soon as he received the letter from the Secretary of the Interior and was now waiting for him. The messenger had returned with the news that Berriman would be by to see him at four o'clock, and it was nearly that now.

Condon poured himself a second drink and was just lifting it to his lips when the door to his office opened and Berriman came in.

"See here, Condon," Berriman said angrily. "How dare you send a messenger to me, demanding that I come see you? There is enough talk about my profiting from the water project as it is. If it gets out that you and I are in collusion, the situation can get much worse."

How like a grub-worm he looks, Condon thought, studying the round, hairless head of the man in front of him. Condon took his drink, without answering Berriman's outburst.

"Well, you sent for me," Berriman said when Condon

didn't reply. "What is it? What is the problem?"

"What is the problem? I'll tell you what the problem is," Condon answered. He pointed to the letter. "I just got a letter from Mr. Columbus Delano. You do know who he is, don't you? He is the Secretary of the Interior. And he is sending an inspector out here next month."

"So?"

"So? So?" Condon answered, so agitated now that his voice trilled up into falsetto. "What do you suppose is going to happen when the inspector discovers a dam where no dam has been authorized?"

"Give him the same story you've been giving the ranchers," Berriman said easily. "Just tell him that you had to dam Gypsum River off because it was diverting too much water from the Colorado River."

"He won't believe that."

"He'll have to believe it," Berriman said. "It will be up to you to convince him."

"That's just it," Condon said. "I'm afraid, if he starts asking me questions, I don't know if I can handle it."

"Don't be such a nervous Nellie and you'll handle it just fine," Berriman said. Berriman smiled and took out his pipe, then, very slowly and deliberately, began tamping the bowl. It was as if, by that action, he was able to calm the fears of Condon, and he took a few seconds attending to his task before he spoke again. And when he did speak, he spoke in a measured, calm voice.

"After all," he said, lighting his pipe and taking audible puffs in between words. "The only real troublemaker around here is Robin Westbury. And I have a feeling that we won't be having any more problems with him. Very soon now, he's going to have more trouble than he can handle, and he's not going to have time to worry about the dam, water rights, or anything else."

"What are you talking about?" Condon asked. "What kind of trouble?"

Berriman clenched the mouthpiece of the pipe in his teeth and smoke encircled his head as he answered Condon's question.

"The very worst kind of trouble a cattleman can have," Berriman said mysteriously. "And if I were you, I wouldn't want to know any more about it."

"I don't, I don't," Condon said, holding up his hands. "But, Mr. Berriman, what are we going to do about this?" He pointed to the letter.

"I can't be bothered with that right now," Berriman answered. "When the time comes, I'm certain you will handle it."

"But I was counting on you for that, Mr. Berriman. I went way out on a limb for you, and I'm counting on your help."

Berriman stood up to leave Condon's office, but before

he left, he looked back at Condon and pointed at him with his pipe. "Condon, when it gets right down to it, I've already paid you for your services. A little sum of ten thousand dollars, I believe, for which you were so gracious as to sign a receipt."

"Oh, my God, the receipt!" Condon said, putting his hand over his mouth. "I had forgotten that you made me sign that foolish thing. Please, you mustn't ever let anyone see that! That could put me in prison!"

"Yes, it could, couldn't it?" Berriman said blandly. "I should think that would be enough incentive to ensure that the government inspectors cause us no problems. Now, you find a way to handle it yourself, Condon, and quit crying to me. I'm out of this deal entirely. I bought myself out when I paid you the money." Berriman smiled. "Good day, Condon."

Chapter Fourteen

It was the middle of the night when Will heard the conversation taking place in the corral. He fought against the intrusion into his sleep, but the persistent voices continued.

"All I'm askin' is that you ride out with me an' take a look," Mo was saying. "I'm tellin' you, there's somethin' wrong."

"It's four o'clock in the mornin'," Choctaw's voice replied gruffly. "I ain't ridin' out at four o'clock in the mornin', just 'cause one of the nighthawks has found a few sick cows."

"Will?" Gid's voice came from the dark. "Will, you awake?"

"Yeah," Will answered. "I am now."

"What do you think is going on?"

"I don't know, but I'm going to find out." Will pulled on his pants, then his boots.

"Yeah, wait a minute, I'm goin' with you," Gid said.

The two men dressed very quickly, then stepped outside to join the two men who were having the conversation. Choctaw was in his long Johns, as if just rousted from his bed. Mo, who was fully dressed, was standing in front of his horse, holding the reins.

"What's going on?" Will asked. "What are you doing in here, Mo? I thought you were ridin' nighthawk tonight."

"I am," Mo answered. "That is, I was, till I saw somethin' I thought Choctaw might want to take a look at. But he don't seem none too interested," he added with a derisive look at the foreman.

"You want somebody to go look at the cows with you, take these two," Choctaw said, taking in Will and Gid with a wave of his hand. "They're the ones Westbury hired to take care of trouble. And it seems to me like what you're talkin' about is trouble."

"You're mighty damn right. If it's what I think it is, it could be big trouble," Mo said. "And bein' as you're the foreman, it seems to me that, by rights, you should be the one goin' out to see about it. Either you or Mr. Westbury."

"No matter what it is, there ain't nothin' I could do about it at this time of night. And whatever it is you found, or you think you found, will still be there come daylight. I'll take a look at it then," Choctaw said. He started back toward the bunkhouse, from which could be heard the sound of a dozen or more snoring sleepers.

"I'll be damned," Mo said as Choctaw walked away. "Never thought I'd see him do anything like that."

"What is the problem, Mo?" Will asked.

"Is it true, what Choctaw said? Are you two boys lookin' out for trouble for Mr. Westbury?"

"I reckon you could say that," Gid answered.

"Well, I don't know as there's anything you can do about this bit of trouble," Mo said. "But the boss needs to know about it, and since Choctaw won't come take a look at it, maybe you boys will."

"Sure, we'll ride out with you," Will said.

They didn't speak during the ride. Mo was a man of few words, and Will knew that he preferred to show him the problem, whatever it was, rather than tell him about it.

Finally, after a ride of some six or seven miles, and with a faint light beginning to crack in the east, they reached a small herd of no more than a hundred or so cows.

"What is it?" Will asked. "What did you want to show us?"

Mo sat in his saddle, looking out over the small herd. Then he saw what he was looking for, and, without a word, he pointed.

Will and Gid saw the cow Mo was pointing to. It was drooling from the mouth, and as it walked it would draw up first one foot, then the other.

"What is that?" Will asked. "What's wrong with that cow?" The two brothers dismounted and walked over toward the animal.

"I think I can tell you," Gid said. He kneeled beside the cow and looked at its hooves. On the skin, just above the hooves, there were dozens of blisters.

"Damn, look at this, Will," Gid said, pointing to the right forefoot.

"What is it, Gid?" Will asked. "You know more about these critters than I do."

"I hope I'm wrong, but it looks to me like this cow has hoof-and-mouth disease," Gid answered, standing up and brushing his hands on his pants.

"Yeah, that's what I thought it was too," Mo said. The young cowboy was still mounted. "I told Choctaw, but he didn't seem none too surprised about it."

"What?" Will asked.

"I said I told Choctaw, but he didn't seem none too worried about it. Leastwise, he wasn't worried enough to come out here and check it out."

"That's not what you said," Will said. "You said he didn't seem too surprised."

"Yeah, well, that too, I guess," Mo said. "I mean, well, when I told him he just sort of shrugged his shoulders like as if he was sayin', 'so what?' "

"This hoof-and-mouth disease," Will said. "Is it

pretty bad?"

"Bad? I'll say it's bad," Mo said. "It's bad enough that the entire herd will have to be destroyed, and then buried in quicklime."

"You mean all these cows?" Will asked.

"No, sir, I mean ever' cow Mr. Westbury's got on the place. That's the law."

"Surely there is no call to do all that?" Will asked.

"Yeah, I'm afraid there is," Gid replied with a sigh. "Soon as word gets out about this, Mr. Westbury won't have any choice. He'll be forced to do it."

"Then, there's no need for word of this to ever get out, is there?" Will suggested. "All we have to do is kill that one cow."

"I don't know, Big Brother, that's awful dangerous," Gid protested. "Hoof-and-mouth disease is a bad thing, and if it gets out, it could wipe out every cow in this part of the state. I'd hate to think we were responsible for that."

"I know, but..." Will stopped in mid-sentence, then took a closer look at the infected animal. "I'll be damned. This isn't even one of Mr. Westbury's beeves."

"What do you mean, he ain't one of our'n?" Mo asked in surprise.

"Look at the brand," Will suggested, pointing to the animal's rump. "What brand is that? It sure isn't Mr. Westbury's."

Mo dismounted and walked over to look at the brand. Instead of the familiar *W*, he saw an *S* sitting over a section of a circle, the ends curving upward.

"A Rocking S," Mo said.

"Is the Rocking S nearby?" Will asked.

Mo shook his head. "Not that I know of, and I know prob'ly ever' ranch within a hundred miles in any direction. Never heard of this one."

"How did a cow from a ranch that's nowhere around here get here?" Will asked.

"And a diseased one at that," Gid added.

Will snapped his fingers. "Son of a bitch," he said. "Gid, I know where this cow came from."

"I think I do too," Gid said. "It was the other night, wasn't it?"

Will nodded his head. "Yes. It wasn't rustlers we spooked. We thought we scared them away, but they didn't come to steal any cows. They did exactly what they intended to do, and that is put this cow into the herd."

"What are you two boys talkin' about?" Mo asked.

Quickly, Will explained how he and Gid had spent the night watching the herd a few days before. He told him, also, about seeing a couple of riders, then running them off.

"We thought they were tryin' to put a leading steer into the herd to take some cows off with it," Gid said. "But there isn't one bit of doubt in my mind but that those two riders, whoever they were, left this cow."

"My God, who would do somethin' like that?" Mo asked. "Don't they know they could infect the entire herd?"

Will nodded. "They not only knew it," he said, "that's *why* they did it."

"Berriman," Gid snorted.

"That would be my guess," Will said.

"Hold on there," Mo said. "Mr. Berriman, he's got cows of his own. Why would he want to go and infect an entire herd?"

"Because he wants Camelot," Will replied. "And he figures that if he wipes out Westbury's herd, Westbury won't be able to go on."

"What pisses me off is the son of a bitch is going to get away with it," Gid snarled.

"Maybe not," Will replied.

"Will, we've got no choice," Gid said. "Mr. Westbury's herd is going to have to be destroyed."

"I agree with you as far as these animals are concerned," Will said. "They have been exposed and they are going to have to be killed. But we may be able to save the rest of the herd."

"How?" Gid asked. "And how are we going to kill this many cows without arousing some suspicion?"

Will shook his head. "I'm afraid I don't have an

answer to that question."

"I have an idea," Mo suggested. "About how we could kill just these cows, I mean."

"How?"

Mo pointed to a steep cliff which formed one side of a nearby gully. About halfway up the cliff a large rock jutted out from the side. It seemed to be positioned to hold back the top half of the wall.

"What do you think would happen if we put some blastin' powder right there under that rock?" he asked.

"It would bring down that entire side," Will said.

"And with the cows trapped in the draw below, it would kill them and bury them at the same time," Gid said, picking up on it as well. "Mo's right, Will, it would work."

"All right, let's do it," Will said.

"God, I'm goin' to hate killin' all them cows like that," Mo said. "It's almost like murder."

"We're going to have to kill them anyway, Mo, you said so yourself," Will said. "Don't look at it as to how many cows we might kill. Look at it as to how many we can save."

"I know you're right," Mo admitted. "I just hate it that we have to do it, that's all."

"And I hate the sons of bitches that caused this," Gid growled.

"Listen, we're going to have to keep them together until

we can set the powder," Will said. "Gid, you think you and Mo could drive them in there, then build a little barricade that will keep them from wandering back out?"

"Yeah, we can do that," Gid said, answering for himself and Mo.

"All right, you two do that, and I'll ride back to the ranch and see if I can find some powder."

"They's some kegs of blasting powder in a shed out behind the barn," Mo said.

"What if Choctaw sees you taking the powder?" Gid asked. "What will you tell him?"

"I'll tell him we're blasting out a well," Will suggested.

The ride to the ranch and back took an hour, and by the time Will returned he saw that Gid and Mo had done their job well. The cattle had been herded into the gully, and a barricade of rocks, limbs, and sagebrush kept them securely pinned inside.

"Gid!" Will called. "Where are you?"

"They're up here with me, Mr. Crockett," a strange voice answered, and Will, startled by the outside voice, reined up sharply. Ahead he saw four men riding down the side of the hill toward him. Three of the men were wearing badges and carrying rifles. The fourth was wearing a suit. Behind the four men, he saw Gid and Mo, and the expressions on their faces showed anger and frustration.

"Who the hell are you?" Will asked the man wearing the suit.

"My name is Edmondson, Dr. Clark Edmondson. I am a veterinarian."

"A veterinarian? We didn't send for a veterinarian."

"I daresay you didn't," Edmondson said. "And from the looks of things, you would have, no doubt, preferred that I not come."

"What are you doing out here?" Will asked.

"I am doing my duty, sir. I was told by an anonymous source that there may be a danger of hoof-and-mouth exposure on Camelot so I rode out here to see for myself."

"You must have left in the middle of the night to get here," Will said. "Do you put that much store in something an anonymous source told you?"

"I assure you, sir, I have as much disdain for an anonymous source as do you. But such an allegation is too serious to overlook. And, in this case, I see that the allegation was correct," Edmondson replied. "I have found one cow that is in the advanced stages of the disease."

"And did you, by chance, notice that the cow was wearing a different brand?" Will asked.

"Yes, your brother pointed that out to me. He also suggested that the cow might have been purposely put into the herd."

"No *might* have been to it, Dr. Edmondson. It *was*

put into the herd," Will said. "Someone has deliberately set about to infect Mr. Westbury's cows."

"I'm sorry, but that doesn't change anything. The animals still must be destroyed."

"I know," Will said with a sigh. He pointed to the two kegs of blasting powder he had brought with him. "That's why we were going to destroy these animals."

"Not just these animals," Edmondson said. "According to the law, you are going to have to destroy every animal on the ranch."

"That law doesn't make any sense," Will said. He pointed toward the east. "This is a big ranch, and the cows are scattered in small bunches all over the place. Hell, some of Berriman's cows are closer to this herd than the rest of Westbury's animals."

Edmondson looked at Will for a moment, then he stroked his chin, as if he were deep in thought.

"Yes," he finally said. "Yes, you do have a point there. All right, I am taking a terrible risk, but, for now, destroy these cows only."

"Thanks," Will answered with a sigh of relief.

"But we are going to keep a very close watch on all the rest of the animals," Edmondson went on. "In no way shall any of them be allowed to come into contact with animals from beyond the boundaries of this ranch."

"That could be a problem," Gid said.

"In what way?" Dr. Edmondson asked. "All you have to do is keep Westbury's cows on the ranch and not let any other cows come into contact with them."

"That's where the problem is," Will said. "As you may know, Berriman has dammed up Gypsum River, cutting all the other ranchers off from a source of water. Mr. Westbury is letting his neighbors bring their cows onto Camelot."

"And they've been doing that all along?" Edmondson asked.

"Yes," Will said. "Of course, some of them are going onto the Double-Diamond and paying Berriman a third of their cows to use his water."

"Wait a minute," Edmondson said, holding up his hand. "Are you telling me that some ranchers bring their cows over here to water, then those same cows might go onto the Double-Diamond?"

"They not only go over there, a third of them stay there," Will said.

"My God," Edmondson said. "With that kind of intermixing of the herds, the entire range has been exposed! I had no idea of the magnitude of this. If we do things to the letter of the law, we would have to slaughter tens of thousands. That would be a catastrophe of unimaginable proportions."

"Then we're going to have to find some other way

of handling it," Will suggested. He pointed to the kegs of powder. "What if we just close off this gully like we were planning?"

"No, no," Edmondson said, shaking his head. "We can't get away with that."

"So what are you plannin' on doin', Doc? Killin' ever' cow in the panhandle?" Mo asked.

"No," Edmondson replied. He pinched the bridge of his nose. "No, I don't want to do that either." Mumbling to himself, he started back toward his horse. Just before he mounted, he turned around to look at Will and the others. "I'll see what I can work out. In the meantime, we can't take a chance on any of these cows getting out, so go ahead and take care of them just as you planned."

"Edmondson?" Will called as the doctor mounted and started to ride away. Edmondson stopped and looked back toward him.

"You're a good man," Will said.

"My intentions are good," Edmondson replied. "Let's just hope that the results aren't disastrous."

Chapter Fifteen

Dr. Clark Edmondson was a graduate of the school of veterinary medicine at Cornell University. He had served in the Federal Army during the Civil War, and at the end of the war found himself in Texas. Unlike so many other ex-Yankees and carpetbaggers who stayed in the defeated South because they saw opportunity there, Dr. Clark Edmondson stayed because he fell in love with Texas. He was entranced by the wide-open spaces, the rugged but beautiful country, and the men and women who were as tough as the country they inhabited. And, as a veterinarian, he felt that he could be of some benefit to his adopted home.

Now all of that, his love of the state, his sense of duty, and his eagerness to do well, was under fire.

At one point during his time in the army Edmondson was put in charge of procuring and certifying the health of every mount in the entire U.S. Cavalry. He was sure he would never again face a responsibility so great. But the responsibility he faced now at least equaled, and perhaps surpassed that. The law, regarding what he should do, was very clear. But the framers of the law could never have anticipated a situation where all the cattle of all the ranchers were so intermixed.

Arguing for some leniency, Dr. Edmondson carried the plight of the ranchers to the Texas Cattle Commission. There, after a long consultation and several detailed negotiations, the Cattle Commission agreed to grant Edmondson the flexibility he sought. Not every animal would have to be killed. However, and this was where the onus came down on Edmondson, every animal known to be or suspected to be directly exposed to the disease would have to be destroyed.

"You understand, do you not, Doctor, that the fate of an entire industry depends upon your good judgment?" the head of the Commission charged.

"I understand, sir," Edmondson replied. "And you may rest assured that I will do my duty."

Although the Texas Cattle Commission granted a waiver which saved many thousands of head of cattle, the number of animals that would have to be destroyed was still quite significant. When Edmondson issued the order it had a tremendous effect upon not only the ranchers, but everyone whose livelihood directly or indirectly depended upon the ranchers. And, in this part of Texas, that was everyone.

The destroy order as it pertained to Camelot included the small herd that Will, Gid, and Mo had already killed and buried in the gully, as well as three more nearby herds. The final count of Robin Westbury's animals to be disposed of was a little over six hundred head. In addition, approximately one hundred cows from Frank Cyrus's herd, and another one hundred from Wilbur Caswell's were included, plus an aggregate of just under a hundred from all the other ranchers who had, to a lesser degree, accepted Westbury's offer of water. The order also called for five hundred head of Double-Diamond cattle to be slaughtered.

Once the notifications went out, all the ranchers who were so notified were called to a meeting in the assembly room of the Cattlemen's Association, located behind the bank, in Loraine.

"By God, I don't mind tellin' you fellas, losing a hundred head of cattle is just about gonna to do me in," Frank Cyrus complained to the others.

"Hell, Frank, by rights you should only have to give up sixty-six head," Wilbur Caswell suggested.

"What do you mean?"

"Ain't Berriman takin' a third of your action?" he asked.

The other ranchers laughed, and even Frank got a chuckle out of the black humor.

"Yeah, how about that, Berriman? Suppose I give you sixty-six cows and you give up the rest?"

"I'm givin' up enough of my own cattle," Berriman answered, not joining in the laughter. "Five hundred cows at forty dollars a head is twenty thousand dollars. And all because, out of the goodness of my heart, I granted you and some of my neighbors access to water."

"You ain't grantin' anybody anything," Wilbur said. "What you're doing is charging them for water that you stole. And as far as I'm concerned you got what's comin' to you. The only thing I regret is that you ain't havin' to destroy your entire herd."

Berriman glared at Wilbur but said nothing.

"Westbury, is it true that the cow that brought the disease in was wearin' a strange brand, one that ain't from around here?'" one of the smaller ranchers asked.

"Yes," Westbury replied. "It was carrying the Rocking S, a brand we have since learned is used by one Mr. Ralph Hardeman, of Dallas."

"Dallas? How did an animal all the way from Dallas get in with your cows?"

"I believe it was purposely introduced," Westbury replied.

"Purposely introduced, you say? What makes you

think that?" Berriman asked.

"A couple of my hands were watching over the herd one night when they encountered what they thought were rustlers," Westbury said. "They shot at them and ran them off. Then later they realized that they weren't trying to rustle at all, but were, instead, putting the infected cow in with my herd."

"These hands you are talking about, they aren't working cowboys, are they?" Berriman asked.

"They work for me," Westbury answered without being more specific.

"But they aren't cowboys?" Berriman repeated.

"They are jacks-of-all-trades. They repair equipment, dig wells, and protect my daughter. They are what the railroad people call troubleshooters."

"It is true, is it not, that in 'protecting' your daughter, they killed four men?"

"Yes," Westbury agreed hesitantly. "But it is my understanding that they had no choice. And they did bring my daughter back safely to me."

"They are gunmen, aren't they?" Berriman accused.

"Who are you to talk about hiring a gunman?" Wilbur asked. "Ain't it true that you've hired Jude Sampson?"

"Yes, what about that?" one of the others asked. "What is Sampson, if he ain't a gunman?"

"What makes you think Sampson is a gunman?"

Berriman asked.

"He killed two of my men," Wilbur said.

"In self-defense," Berriman replied.

"That's a bunch of bull," Wilbur thundered. "That no-lip son of a bitch goaded them into drawing on him. Hell, all the witnesses say as much."

"Those same eyewitnesses say that your men drew first."

"Now he hangs out in the Cattle Call in town, near about ever' night, tryin' to fight with our hands," another man added.

"Gentlemen," Berriman said in an oil-smooth voice. "If your men are picking fights in the saloons, it is, no doubt, because they are trying to prove something. I would advise them, however, not to attempt to pick a fight with Sampson. Of course he is skilled with a firearm, that's why I hired him. But I didn't hire him as a gunman, nor even as a troubleshooter. I hired him as a bodyguard."

"Bodyguard?"

"Yes, bodyguard. Is that so unusual? It certainly should come as no surprise to you gentlemen to learn that I am a very wealthy man. That means that there are many who would attack me, and rob me, if they could. But as long as Mr. Sampson is in my employ, no one would dare."

Sampson, who had been the object of the spirited discussion, stood over by the wall with his arms folded across his chest. His gun was worn low and kicked out in the way of a gunman, and he was as totally disdainful of the ranchers' discussion of him as if they had been talking about the weather.

"On the other hand, Robin, the two men that you have hired, these Crockett brothers, are quite dangerous indeed. Are you aware that they were members of Quantrill's Raiders? That is the most infamous band of cutthroats and brigands ever assembled."

"I am aware that they fought with Quantrill," Westbury replied. "But I am also aware that there are many in the South who don't consider Quantrill a brigand at all, but rather regard him as a true cavalier for the Confederate cause."

Westbury's response was met with a barrage of cheers from the other ranchers, nearly all of whom had fought in the recent war on the side of the South. Berriman waited until the cheers subsided before he continued his argument.

"Regardless of the perceived merits or faults of the two men in question, they were hired by you to look for trouble. Isn't that right?"

Westbury paused for a moment before he answered. "Yes," he finally said.

"Then don't you think that it's entirely possible that the Crockett brothers might have, themselves, introduced a diseased animal to your herd?"

"No. Why in heaven's name would they do such a thing?"

"Perhaps they thought it would make them look more important in your eyes," Berriman suggested.

"I have no reason to doubt them."

"What is it you are getting' at, Berriman?" Wilbur asked. "Do you have some other idea as to where that animal might have come from?"

"As a matter of fact, I do," Berriman replied.

"Then, by all means, share it with us," Westbury challenged.

"I was waiting for you to ask," Berriman said. He smiled smugly and held up a piece of paper. "Gentlemen, this is a bill of lading. According to this document, Mr. Westbury took receipt, by rail shipment, of twenty head of cattle, four weeks ago. The point of origin for the cattle was Dallas, Texas. And, as we have just been told, the diseased cow came from Dallas, Texas."

There were several exclamations of surprise from the other ranchers, and a few shouted curses and accusations. Dr. Edmondson, who had been conducting the meeting, had to bang the gavel repeatedly to restore order.

"That is a very reckless accusation, Mr. Berriman," Westbury said in an angry, clipped voice.

"What about it, Westbury?" one of the other ranchers called out. "Did you have them cows shipped in or not?"

"Gentlemen, the twenty head of cattle on that bill of lading are all blooded brood bulls. I assure you, the pathetic creature we found on the range would not come under that category."

"Yes, well, how are we going to prove that now?" Berriman asked. "The animal in question has already been conveniently destroyed and disposed of. And no one saw it but your men."

"That's not true," Westbury replied. "Dr. Edmondson also saw it."

"Is that true, Dr. Edmondson?" Homer Cyrus asked. "Did you see the infected cow?"

"Yes, I saw the animal."

"Do you think it was one of the blooded brood bulls Westbury is talking about?"

"It was a bull," Edmondson agreed. "But its condition was so deteriorated that it is difficult to judge as to whether it would have been one of the blooded bulls Mr. Westbury is talking about."

"Oh, come now. You're a veterinarian, ain't you? Are you tellin' me you couldn't tell whether it was a blooded bull or not?" one of the ranchers demanded.

"I'm sorry," Edmondson said. "As I said, its condition was too far gone for me to be able to judge."

"Hell, I don't need you to judge," Homer said. "If Robin Westbury says the diseased animal wasn't one of the cows he shipped in, then that's good enough for me."

"Mr. Cyrus, for your faith and confidence in me, you have my most sincere appreciation," Westbury said.

"Dr. Edmondson, may I make a motion?" one of the other ranchers asked.

"Yes, please do," Edmondson answered. The meeting was becoming difficult.

"If that cow really is from Dallas, it sure as hell didn't walk here. And if it didn't come in with the twenty that Westbury says he bought, then it must've come in by itself. Why don't you check with the railroad and see where it come from, and who it went to."

"I shall do so," Edmondson promised.

"Which brings us right back to where we was," Wilbur said.

"And that is?" Edmondson asked.

"That somebody put that cow onto Camelot for the pure purpose of infecting all of Camelot's cattle."

"Yeah, only when they did it, they got our cows too," one of the other ranchers added.

"So all we need to do now is find out who the bastard is, then string him up!" someone shouted.

"Yeah!" the others responded in a loud yell.

"If you ask me," Wilbur said, "we don't have to look no further than to find out who stands to gain and who stands to lose in this deal."

"Gain? Who could possibly gain from such a thing?" Homer asked.

Wilbur looked directly at Berriman. "Maybe somebody who figures that he can pick up our ranches real cheap if we all lose our herds."

"See here!" Berriman sputtered, pointing at Wilbur. "Are you accusing me? You have no right to say such a thing!"

"I reckon I've got a right to call a skunk a skunk when I see one," Wilbur said. "And if you don't care for my remarks, Berriman, you can always call me out."

"Here, here, hold on now!" Dr. Edmondson shouted, holding his hands up in an effort to quiet the situation. "There's no need for all that. There will be nobody calling anybody out. Now, gentlemen, we have a bad situation facing us here and the only way we are going to get through it is by cooperating with one another. The bad news is, you are going to have to kill some cattle. But the good news is, you don't have to destroy your entire herds."

"Hear, hear," Westbury said. He stood up and looked at the other assembled ranchers. "Gentlemen, regardless of how this diseased animal got onto my ranch, it did get there, and thus exposed not only my cattle but some of yours as well. For that, I deeply apologize. But," he pointed toward Dr. Edmondson, "let us not, in our frustration, lose sight of what Dr. Edmondson has done for us. He has saved thousands of animals from a senseless and wasteful slaughter, and I think we owe him our appreciation, and a round of applause."

The ranchers applauded and, in their common cause, some of the bitterness passed.

"Gentlemen, you all know the arrangement," Edmondson said. "For the most part you will be on your honor. I ask you not to violate that trust, but to bring every cow that you know or even suspect may have been exposed to the field designated on the maps you received when you arrived today. And I thank you in advance for your cooperation."

In order to bring about a more efficient operation, all the affected cattle from all the ranches were gathered in one large, open field on public land. On the day appointed, cowboys from all the ranches drove their herds to the designated place. The operation had all the trappings of a regular spring roundup, and, despite the solemnity of the occasion, there was a sense of excitement to the event. As Will and Gid approached they could hear the sounds of the drive, the bawling and crying of cattle, and the shouts and whistles of the wranglers before they could actually make anything out in the dust cloud.

Finally they could see the cows moving forward relentlessly, prodded on by the drovers. The two brothers rode around the edge of the growing herd, keeping out of everyone's way as they headed for the chuck wagon. The chuck wagon, they knew, would be the headquarters of the drive, and there they saw Dr. Edmondson and several of his assistants making a careful inventory, by owner, of all the cows that were brought in.

The count served two purposes. It would assess the amount of damage done by the outbreak, and it would also determine the compensation to be paid to the cattle-men for the animals they were forced to destroy. Though the compensation was minuscule compared to the losses they were actually sustaining, it was a source of badly needed revenue for some of the smaller ranchers.

By early afternoon more than a hundred men, dressed in long white coats and wearing bandannas, were ready to go about the grim work of slaughter. This impromptu army was composed of cowboys from all the ranches except those that were affected.

"You boys about ready?" Dr. Edmondson called to them.

The lead cowboy, a foreman from a ranch in the next county, nodded, then jacked a round into the chamber of his rifle and started toward the herd.

"Let's go, boys," he called to the others.

There was the sound of a score or more rifles being cocked, then, a moment later, the first bang.

Immediately after the first shot came a dozen more,

then more yet, so that it quickly took on the sound of a battlefield, with rifles roaring, men shouting, cattle bawling then falling over.

Gun smoke drifted over the tightly gathered herd, and the smell of expended powder joined the odor of cow manure and the sickeningly sweet smell of fear.

The cowboys who had brought the cattle in, the same ones who had rounded them up as calves, branded them, and worked them for the past few years, now stood by and watched the killing. Their faces were pinched, their eyes squinted, and they smoked, or stood by in silence, deploring what was going on but unable to take their eyes off the massacre.

The killing went on with grim efficiency. The animals would be shot, then dragged into one of several large pits which had been dug nearby. The pits were lined with lime, and as the cows were tossed into the pits they too would be covered with lime.

Like the other hands from Camelot, Will and Gid were taking no part in the actual slaughter, but were standing near the chuck wagon, watching silently. Dr. Edmondson came over to draw himself a cup of coffee, then he turned to watch as the shooting continued.

"Gruesome business, this," Edmondson said.

"Yeah," Gid grunted.

"All the more gruesome when you realize that it was a

deliberate attempt to infect the herd," Edmondson said. He pulled a letter from his jacket pocket. "I got this letter from Mr. Hardeman this morning, confirming that he was, indeed, the source of the diseased cow."

Gid looked at him in surprise. "What? You mean the son of a bitch admitted it?"

"He admits shipping the cow out here by rail."

"Who did he send it to?" Will asked.

"Yes, well, now that is the mystery," Edmondson answered. "Mr. Hardeman claims he was contacted by a representative of West Texas Normal and offered top dollar for a hoof-and-mouth infected animal to be used in their college of veterinary medicine for research."

"Where is West Texas Normal?"

"That's just it," Edmondson replied. "There is no such school."

"All right, who picked up the cow at the depot?"

Edmondson shook his head. "I wasn't able to get an answer to that question," he said. "I checked. The freight master remembers seeing the bill of lading, but, according to his records, the cow was never claimed. Whoever got it must've sneaked down to the train yard in the middle of the night and taken it off the car. I'd sure like to find out who it was."

"Yeah," Will said menacingly. "I'd like to find out too."

"Dr. Edmondson," someone called, "you want to come

over here a minute?"

"Would you gentlemen excuse me, please?" Edmondson asked as he left to respond to the call. As Edmondson was leaving, Mo Eubanks came over to pour himself a cup of coffee. Mo was one of the cowboys who had brought in the Camelot herd.

"Listen to them sons of bitches," Mo growled, taking in the shooters with a wave of his arm. "By God, I think some of those bastards are actually enjoying this. Listen to 'em yell."

Mo was referring to the frequent "yahoos!" and occasional Rebel yells that could be heard through the incessant banging of the rifles.

"They think it's like hunting buffalo or something," Mo said.

"It could've been worse," Will said.

"Yeah, I guess so. My God, can you imagine if we'd had to kill every cow on the place? And the other ranches besides?" Mo replied. He took a swallow of coffee and looked out toward the herd.

Suddenly a steer broke loose from the herd and dashed through the line of shooters, heading at a dead run toward the chuck wagon.

"Stop him! Get him!" someone shouted.

Mo leaped into the saddle of his horse and started after the steer. Bringing his horse right alongside the terrified critter, he leaned over from his saddle, then, grabbing the animal by the horns, leaped from his horse. Digging his boots into the ground he let the steer drag him for a few feet, then the animal came to a stop and Mo twisted its neck around, bringing it down.

Shortly after that Burt Thompson arrived with a rope. He threw the rope to Mo, and Mo dropped it around the steer's head so it could be led back into the herd.

"Wait a minute!" Mo called, just before Burt started back toward the herd with it.

"What is it?" Burt asked.

"Look at this ear," Mo said, pointing to the animal's ear. "Ain't this ..." Mo stopped and looked at the brand. "No, it can't be," he said. "Still, it..."

"Burt! Get that cow back with the others!" Choctaw suddenly shouted.

"Choctaw, this here cow looks like ..." Mo started, but by now Choctaw had ridden over, and he took the lariat from Burt, then put his horse into a gallop, forcing the steer to run back into the herd.

"Shoot this son of a bitch before it runs away again!" Choctaw shouted, and the closest shooter brought the steer down with one shot.

Choctaw rode back to Mo, who was still standing there, looking on in surprise at the foreman's odd behavior.

"I don't know what you saw, or think you saw," Choctaw growled. He pointed back toward the herd. "But whatever it was, forget about it. We're out here to see to it that them cows gets killed. Now, if you ain't quite got the stomach for it, you go on back to the ranch."

"I was just—" Mo started.

"I don't care what you was just," Choctaw interrupted. "These men have a hard-enough job to do without you getting' in their way."

Choctaw slapped his legs against the sides of his horse and galloped away, headed for a distant part of the herd.

Duly chastised, Mo remounted, then rode back over to the chuck wagon, from which Will and Gid had witnessed the entire scene.

"Good job of bulldogging the steer," Gid offered, as Mo dismounted.

"Thanks," Mo replied. He looked sullenly toward Choctaw, who was now small in the distance. "I sure as hell don't know what he was all riled up over."

"What were you talking about?" Will asked.

"That's just it," Mo said. "I didn't get a chance to talk at all. But if I had, I would've pointed out somethin' that's a mite peculiar."

"What's that?"

"That steer I just run down had a strange right ear. Actually, you might say it had three strange right ears."

"Three ears? What are you talking about?"

"The right ear," Mo said. "It ain't one ear at all. It's three separate, very small, but perfectly formed ears. I remember seeing it when I branded it as a calf a couple of years ago." He laughed. "I recall that me 'n Percy was goin' to see if we could buy 'im off Mr. Westbury. We was goin' to take 'im back east and show 'im off at county fairs an' the like, then get rich."

"And that's one of 'em we're havin' to kill," Gid said. "I'm sorry."

"No, that ain't it," Mo said. "Well, that too, but the funny thing about that cow was the brand it was wearin'."

"What about the brand?"

"It was a Double-Diamond brand," Mo said. "I know damn well that was the same cow. What I don't know is why it was wearin' the Double-Diamond brand."

"Hey, Mo, you wanna give us a hand over here?" someone called, and Mo excused himself and went over to offer his assistance to the cowboy who had called him.

Will waited until Mo and the others were gone, then he squatted down and picked up a stick and started scratching in the dirt.

"What are you doin'?" Gid asked.

"Look at this," Will replied.

Will scratched a *W* in the dirt. "What is that?" he asked.

"It's a W. Camelot's brand," Gid said.

"Yes. Now, look at this." Will stood up, then walked

around to the other side of the *W* he had scratched in the ground. He made another *W,* but from the opposite direction. The second *W* he put right on top of the first.

"What do you think it is now?" he asked.

"I'll be damned," Gid answered, looking at the brand his brother had just completed drawing. "It's the Double-Diamond."

Chapter Sixteen

Mollie dipped a cloth in the bucket of water, then began washing the blackboards in the single-room schoolhouse. The woman who had taught school the year before had gotten married during the summer, and the Loraine school board offered the job to Mollie. Mollie took it, not so much from the need of an income, as a need to keep herself gainfully occupied.

The job also provided a small living quarters at the back of the school, and although Mollie had enjoyed her stay with Victoria, she was looking forward to a place of her own.

She covered the board with broad sweeps, watching the slate grow black under each pass as the white film of chalk was cleaned away.

Across the street from the school, Jude Sampson stood just inside the livery stable. The bottom half of the door was closed and he leaned on it, looking through the open top half. From here, he had discovered, he could see into the school, and he could watch Mollie Vitters, without her knowing she was being watched.

In the week since Mollie Vitters had moved to town and begun preparation for the start of school, she had spoken to Sampson only in the most perfunctory way. Sometimes he would watch carefully, judging exactly when she would leave the school, then he would hurry to get into position to walk by her. He always made it a point to tip his hat and speak, and she answered him with a polite nod of her head, but never once had they exchanged any pleasantries.

Who does she think she is? He wondered. Men quaked in their boots when he spoke to them. He once made a six-foot-tall, powerfully built man get on his knees and beg for his life. Even now, as he recalled that moment, he relished the thought of reducing such a fine specimen of manhood to a quivering lump of jelly.

Then he blew his brains out.

"You are in that schoolhouse all alone some evenin's, ain't you, missy?" Sampson said under his breath. "Well, little miss high-and-mighty bitch, let's see what you're like some late night when you think you're safe, when there's nobody around for you to turn to. I'll just pay you a visit, and you'll notice me then. Yes, ma'am, I can guarantee that you will notice me.

"The first thing I'm going to do is make sure that you know I'm the one who killed your uncle. Then after you learn that little bit of information, I'll tell you what I have planned for you.

"You'll beg me not to kill you. You'll offer to let me use you any way I want. But all your beggin' and all your offers won't do you any good.

"No, ma'am, It won't do you any good a'tall."

Back at Camelot, Victoria stood in her room at the mirror and studied her reflection. How different her world was here from what it had been in England. There she had been a schoolgirl with only the most remote notion of life. Now she was experiencing life to its fullest.

And yet one thing persisted.

As an English schoolgirl her life was orderly and ordered. She knew exactly who she was and what her station in life was. She never thought about men except in some vague, romantic way, taken from novels of knights in shining armor rescuing fair young damsels.

She never thought that *she* would be rescued by some knight in shining armor, because her own future was already planned. She was engaged to Sir Jeremy Bathurst, son of the Duke of Wharncliff. Sir Jeremy was actually her second cousin, and the marriage had been arranged by her father and the Duke of Wharncliff when she was only twelve years old. She had only seen him once in the last ten years.

Although Sir Jeremy was her fiancé, and as far as she knew, the arrangement was still in effect, Victoria never thought of him in any sort of erotic way. Not in the way she thought of Will Crockett. Oh, how wonderful it would be, she thought, if she could marry Will Crockett instead of Sir Jeremy Bathurst.

Of course, that could never be. Will Crockett was a common cowboy ... no, not even a cowboy. He and his brother were drifters, with no more attachment to the land than the tumbleweed the late, hot August winds rolled across the prairie. Victoria was a titled Lady, and even though there were no such things as titles in America, there was, nevertheless, a rigid recognition of the class system. Americans gave lip service to all men being created equal, but money, position, social standing, race, and religion separated Americans into classes as rigidly as did the peerage system in England.

No matter how one looked at it, Will Crockett, a gunman who once rode for Quantrill, a man nearly everyone called a bandit, was not in Victoria's social class. And, even if Victoria would step out of her class for him, she knew, intuitively, that he would never leave his class for her.

Victoria leaned forward to study her face more closely in the mirror. Then, looking deep into her own eyes, she spoke aloud.

"Well, bloody hell, I don't want to marry him. I just want to sleep with him."

She laughed at her own bawdy candidness.

Half an hour later Victoria, already mounted, appeared at the corral. Will was saddling his horse.

"Well, I must say I am hurt," Victoria said.

Will looked around in confusion.

"Beg your pardon?"

"I said I am hurt," Victoria said. "Here, I asked you to take me on a ride around the ranch to show me the location of all the wells, and when I get here, you aren't even ready to go."

Will pulled out the gold pocket watch that had been his father's and looked at it.

"You said two o'clock," he said. "It's five minutes until."

"Oh? Well, then, perhaps I am the anxious one," Victoria said with a little laugh.

Will tightened the cinch, then swung into the saddle and smiled over at her. "All right," he said. "Now let's go."

An hour later, when they were some distance away, a

great billowing rain cloud built up in the west.

"Damn!" Will said. "Isn't this the way of it, though? Here we've been breaking our backs getting in these wells and now it rains."

"Yes, but after the rain is gone and the puddles dry up, the cattle will still be here, and they will still need water," Victoria said.

"You're right about that," Will agreed. "In the meantime, we'd better go look for some shelter somewhere. Sometimes these summer storms can be real humdingers."

Will helped Victoria get her poncho on, then he put his own on and spread them both out to provide as much protection for the horses as he could.

"Let's go," he called out, and he led the way, moving off in a fast trot.

The dark, ominous clouds moved closer to them, preceded by swiftly moving tumbleweed and a rolling column of dust. Will and Victoria leaned forward in their saddles and hurried on.

Moments later the rains came, hitting them full force. At first, Will thought they would try to make it all the way back to the house, but the rain was coming with such velocity that the drops were actually stinging. Then a few minutes after the rain started it began to hail, and the horses grew frightened. That was when Will saw the line shack.

"Over there!" he called against the force of the storm.

Alongside the shack was a small lean-to for the horses, and Will tied them there. Then Will took Victoria by the hand and they darted through the storm to the weather-beaten shack.

"It appears cozy enough," Victoria said once they were inside. "It isn't even leaking."

Will looked around at the little line shack. It had a real tick mattress on the bed, a table and two chairs, and a combination cooking and heating stove. There was also a cabinet with several tins of fruits and vegetables, some dry beans, and coffee.

"They keep it well stocked, don't they?" Victoria said.

"Yes, well, I suppose when someone has to stay out here, he would like it to be as comfortable as possible," Will said.

Will stepped out onto the front porch to watch the rain move across the mesa and slash into the prairie. A prairie dog, driven from one hole by quickly rising water, bounded along through the rain and disappeared down into another.

Though Will was sheltered from the direct effect of the rain, he was being splashed with the spray, but he made no attempt to escape. He liked the rain. It blanketed all sight and sound, and formed a curtain behind which his soul could exist in absolute solitude. Only those with whom he really wanted to share could penetrate it.

The front door opened and Victoria came out onto the porch to join him.

Victoria looked out over the rain-swept prairie. "Oh, I know it is inconvenient," she said. "But I just love the rain. It reminds me of England. It rains often in England."

"Well, it may rain more in England, but I'll bet we have bigger storms," Will said.

"Yes, you do. You have wonderful, glorious storms," Victoria said, and she hugged herself as she leaned out to let some of the rain splash in her face. She laughed, then drew back out of the rain and looked at him, her face now spattered with droplets of water. Their eyes held for a moment, then she put her hand on his face, running her fingers along his jawline.

"Do you know that, in my country, we would never have even had the opportunity to meet?"

"I reckon not, seeing as I've never been to England," Will answered.

Victoria laughed. "No, I don't mean that. I mean if we both lived in England and we were both... as we are now."

Will smiled crookedly. "You mean, you being a princess and me being a peasant?"

"Well, I'm not a princess and you aren't a peasant," Victoria replied with a little laugh. "But, yes, something like that. Maybe we should get in out of the rain."

Will held open the door. "After you, m'lady," he said as he bowed down.

Victoria giggled. "Oh, you do play the game well."

Inside the little line shack, they could hear the rain drumming against the roof and the two windows.

"There's some dry wood," Will said. "Would you like me to get a fire started in the stove?"

"Oh, yes, that would be wonderful."

"Maybe you could make some coffee," Will suggested.

In addition to the dry wood Will found a box of lucifers and soon had a fire going.

Will watched Victoria putter around the kitchen for a moment, and he could tell by her hesitant approach to everything that this was probably all new to her. She had been raised with servants, schooled to the life of ease. He couldn't help but feel a very strong attraction to her, and he knew that the feeling was reciprocated.

While Victoria put on the coffee, Will stepped out onto the porch again.

After a while, the front door opened and Victoria leaned out.

"It's ready," she said.

There were two cups on the table, and Victoria held out her hand in invitation.

When Will sat at the table he picked up the cup, tasted the beverage, then frowned. "This isn't coffee."

"No," Victoria said, smiling brightly. "Isn't it wonderful? I found some tea."

Will took another swallow. "It's all right," he said. "Though, right now, I'd probably drink hot water and be satisfied."

They sat across the table drinking their tea, engaging in small talk. Then Victoria asked the question that was burning inside her.

"Will, do you think there could ever be anything between us? I don't mean some furtive assignation. I mean something real."

Will took another sip of his tea and looked across his cup at Victoria. She was, truly, a beautiful woman and though he couldn't call up the word to describe it, he could sense her vulnerability.

"Victoria, you said it yourself," he replied, speaking quietly. "We don't have lords and ladies here but we do have differences. The life you live, and the life I live are as different as night and day."

Victoria didn't answer, but Will saw tears welling up in her eyes.

"The Indians have a saying for something like this," Will continued. "A fish and a bird may marry, but where will they live?"

"I know," she said. She reached across the table to take his hand. "Believe me, I know."

They said nothing for a long moment until Will noticed that the rain which had driven them inside seeking shelter was over.

"The rain has stopped," he finally said. "We should get back."

"Will?" There was a subtle change in the tone of her voice, as if realization and resignation had sunk in. She smiled. "Am I the fish or the bird?"

"Definitely the bird."

Victoria kissed Will on the cheek, then made a little face. "I've been meaning to tell you," she said. "You really should shave more often."

Chapter Seventeen

The rain, which had been falling intermittently through-out the day, began again that night. In her room at the rear of the schoolhouse, Mollie had already gone to bed. She lay there listening to the rain, watching the flash-es of lightning through the window, shrinking before the crashing reports of thunder. Then, in between the thunder and the roar of rain, she heard a banging sound from the front of the schoolhouse. She lay still for a full moment longer, trying to ignore it, but she knew she couldn't. If the door had blown open she was going to have to close it right away. School would be starting soon, and she couldn't afford to have her books ruined by the rain.

With a sigh, Mollie got up to investigate the source of the sound.

At first she thought she would take a candle. Then she decided she didn't want to waste the match. Besides, she had been working here now for the past two weeks, and she knew the classroom well enough to navigate it with her eyes closed.

The thunder boomed and the rain roared as Mollie walked from her room, passing through the children's cloakroom, and out into the classroom. She stayed against the wall so as not to bump into any of the students' desks, and started picking her way toward the front door.

Halfway there, she stopped.

She hadn't heard or seen anything, but for some strange reason she began to experience the uneasy sensation that she wasn't alone. Her hair stood on end, and a hollowness began spreading from the pit of her stomach.

"Hello?" she called out tentatively. She waited for a moment but got no answer. "Hello, who's there?" she called again.

Still no answer.

The feeling grew stronger, and the uneasiness turned to outright fear.

"I know someone is here," she said, her voice nearly breaking. "Who is it? What do you want? If you are just looking to get out of the rain, please tell me. You are frightening me."

Suddenly there was a brilliant flash of lightning, a large bolt that illuminated everything for fully two seconds. The entire classroom was brightly lit, a world without color. She could see every object in the room with amazing clarity. She saw each desk standing out in bold relief, and the alphabet she had so carefully copied on the blackboard.

And she could see Sampson, standing just inside the door. With his teeth protruding through the part of his lib that was missing, he took on the appearance of an apparition from the bowels of hell itself.

The room went instantly black. Mollie screamed, but her scream was drowned out by the crash of thunder that came immediately after the light died.

"Come here, bitch!" Sampson shouted. He started to run toward her, but in the dark, he hit his shin and tripped over one of the desks. He fell, cursing, to the floor.

Mollie turned to run but stopped short of going into her room. She couldn't go in there because there was no door leading out and she would be trapped. The only way out of the building was by the front door, but she couldn't go that way without passing Sampson. Mollie got down on her hands and knees and started crawling, quickly, along the floor. She was just below the blackboard, and it was her intention to hide behind her desk.

No, she couldn't go there. That would be the first place he'd look!

She had to think!

She couldn't just go pell-mell around the room, she

had to have some destination, some purpose! She had the presence of mind then to remember that there was a loose board right in front of her, so she moved around it, then crawled through the darkness to the opposite wall.

"Where are you, whore?" Sampson called, his sibilant voice sounding like the hiss of a serpent. "I've got something for you." He giggled insanely. Another flash of lightning, neither as brilliant nor as long as the previous flash, lit the room dimly. From her position on the floor near the bookshelves, Mollie could see that Sampson was now holding a gun.

The light frightened her and she moved sharply, bumping into the shelf and knocking several books onto the floor. Sampson heard her and looked over just as the light was dying. He got a fleeting glimpse of her and he fired, the flash from his pistol extending the illumination of the room for a split second.

The bullet crashed into a shelf near her, and splinters of wood flew from the impact. One little sliver hit her in the arm and she felt its sting.

"You can't get away from me," Sampson called. He began moving across the room toward her, stumbling into one desk after another, cursing with each new obstacle.

Mollie crawled quickly along the wall, heading toward the door.

"I made it easy for your uncle," Sampson said. "I

killed him quick."

"You ... you killed him?" Mollie gasped. She bit her tongue, for she realized, instantly, that she should have made no sound. But it was impossible not to react to Sampson's almost casual comment about killing her uncle.

Sampson smiled broadly. He had gotten just the response he wanted, and hearing her voice located her for him.

"Yeah, I killed him," he continued, baiting her. 'But, like I said, I made it easy for him. He didn't suffer none. He died just real quick. If you're nice to me, I'll make it easy for you, too."

"Why did you kill my uncle? What did he ever do to you?"

This time Mollie planned her comment, for as soon as she spoke, she crawled backward several feet, hoping to make him think she was in one place when actually she was in another.

"Because I like to kill," Sampson replied. "And I like killin' women even more. Killin' a woman is the same as beddin' a woman. 'N killin' a purty woman pleasures me even more."

Mollie tried to turn around, to go back to the front of the room again, but when she did, she knocked over some more books. They fell with a series of loud thuds, once again giving away her position.

Sampson fired again, shooting blindly in the direction of the sound. Ironically, he was closer this time than he was previously, and Mollie could feel the concussion of the bullet whizzing by, frying the air just in front of her before it slammed into the wall.

"If you want, I can kill you fast," Sampson said. "Course, I like it more when I can hurt you a little, 'n you got time to be a' scared knowin' you're about to die. But slow or fast, it don't make that much of a never mind to me. Dead or alive, I'll get my pleasure from you."

From the position of his voice, Mollie realized a small glimmer of hope. He was moving aimlessly through the room, which might give her a chance to get out. She started crawling toward the door.

"What you tryin' to do, girl? You think you can make it outside?" Sampson asked. He moved again and Mollie's heart fell, as she could hear him moving back into a blocking position. "Yeah, you do that. You try an' make it to the door. I'll just be here, waitin' on you."

Another streak of lightning. The room flashed white, and she could see him standing no more than a few feet from her. Then it grew dark once more, and the thunder boomed.

Driven by terror now, Mollie made a desperate run toward the door, but Sampson anticipated it and in one quick lunge, caught her, then spun her around. In what was almost a reflex action, Mollie's hand reached up and clawed at his face. Her long fingernails opened four deep tracks on his face, and he began bleeding.

"Ow! You bitch!" Sampson shouted. He was still holding his pistol in his hand, and he brought it across the side of her head in a vicious swipe. Mollie saw stars flash as the gun barrel struck her in the side of the head, then she went out.

When she came to a few moments later, he had lit a candle and was looking down at her.

"Good, you're still alive," Sampson said. "I was afraid I'd already kilt you, 'n I wanted you to know what was happenin'. Are you a' scairt?"

"Yes," Mollie replied, barely able to even say the word."

"That's what I wanted," Sampson said. He fired his pistol. The gunshot sounded like thunder, and Mollie felt something hit her hard in the chest.

From a house near the school, a dog began to bark. Sampson took two quick steps toward Mollie's body. Standing over her, he cocked his pistol for a second shot when, outside, more barking dogs joined the first. He thought about it for a moment, then he eased the hammer down and slipped the pistol back into his holster. It wasn't until that moment that he began to feel the pain brought about by Mollie's life-and-death struggling scratch. He took his handkerchief out and held it up to the wound.

"Bitch," he snarled. "I was goin' to finish you off... make it easy for you. But as far as I'm concerned, you can just lay here and die slow."

With dozens of dogs now adding to the cacophony, Sampson slipped out of the door, down the steps, then walked, almost casually, across the street to the livery stable. There he mounted his already saddled horse and rode out into the rain, toward the Double-Diamond. He was in no particular hurry. He knew that the chances of anyone coming out in the rain to see what all the dogs were barking about were remote.

Back inside the schoolhouse, Mollie regained consciousness a second time. She tried to get up but couldn't. Slowly and laboriously, she worked her way across the floor to the blackboard wall. Painfully, she reached up to grab the chalk tray and, using it as an assist bar, started pulling herself up. She was almost erect, when she felt her knees weaken and her legs give way. She fell to the floor again.

As she fell, she made a grab to stop the fall, but succeeded only in pulling down a few pieces of chalk.

Mollie tried to get up again, but she had no strength left, so she just lay there, feeling herself growing weaker. She began moving her hand around in the dark, on the floor, looking for the chalk. Finally she was able to wrap her fingers around a piece of it and laboriously tried to write something on the floor.

She couldn't hold the chalk... she had no strength in her fingers. Twice she started, but she dropped the chalk. Finally, mustering up all the strength and willpower she had remaining, she formed the top part of the first letter.

That was as far as she could go. With strength and willpower gone, her hand trailed away, putting a long, ill-formed tail falling away from the top of the letter.

"I hope I got enough of it," she said. "Please, God," she prayed. "I hope I got enough of it."

Chapter Eighteen

Later that same morning, out at the Double-Diamond, Choctaw found himself standing on the front porch of the big house, holding his hat in his hand as he waited to speak with Berriman. It irritated him that the Mexican woman Berriman had working for him would keep him waiting out on the porch like a panhandler. But he didn't press the issue. He was here to do some business, and he knew that a person couldn't do business if he was argumentative.

Choctaw stepped over to the edge of the porch and looked out over the rolling acres that Berriman had amassed in the few years he had been here since the war. God, what he wouldn't give to own a place just like this.

Choctaw couldn't help but wonder how Berriman, who had come to Texas empty-handed after the war, was able to build such a large and impressive ranch in so short a time. Of course it may have helped that Berriman was a Yankee and knew all the other carpetbaggers. Some said that Berriman was a Yankee officer during the war, and ex-Yankee officers who knew the right people were able to get things done easier than former Rebs, even Rebs who had been officers.

Choctaw had been an officer, a captain in the Texas Cavalry. When the war ended he returned to Texas hardened and feeling betrayed. Despite the fact that the South had lost the war... or perhaps even because of the fact, Choctaw was a man with ambitions. He was going to find some land to homestead, hunt wild cows, and then use the land and cattle as the basis of a ranching empire.

Choctaw had no qualms about what it would take to build his ranch. If he had to throw a long rope now and then, or ride an outlaw trail, then so be it. During the war he had murdered, robbed, pillaged, and burned for the Confederacy. It seemed only right that he should put those well-developed skills to work for himself.

But Choctaw was never able to file the paperwork he needed to take title to the land, and his cow hunts produced only a few miserable specimens, unfit to start a herd. Frustrated by his failure, he finally took a job as foreman for Robin Westbury.

For a while after starting work for Westbury, Choctaw harbored the secret though totally irrational hope that he and Westbury's daughter might get married. If that would happen, then someday Camelot would belong to him. But he learned very quickly that Victoria Westbury had no interest in him.

With no chance of ever inheriting Camelot, Choctaw's next move was to determine how to convert his position as foreman of the ranch into a means of personal profit. That was the first and only plan of his to come to fruition, when he discovered a secret pass that led to a connecting valley between Camelot and Double-Diamond. It was a valley that, while sheltered from casual observation, could hide several hundred head of cattle.

This presented him with a golden opportunity, but before Choctaw did anything about it, he visited Berriman and showed him how easily he could convert Camelot's brand, which was a *W* for Westbury, into the brand of two connected diamonds, used by Double-Diamond. He then offered to provide Berriman with these brand-altered cattle at a bargain price. Berriman accepted the offer, and for the last six months, Choctaw and Rad, the one cowboy he had recruited from Camelot, rustled cows from Westbury and sold them to Berriman.

Although that provided Choctaw with an additional source of income, he hit upon another way to make money. Recruiting four out-of-work drifters, men who had served with him during the war, he arranged to have them abduct Victoria Westbury. It had been his intention to hold Victoria for a ransom of twenty thousand dollars. That was a small fortune, but he knew that Robin Westbury not only had that much money, but would readily give it to get his daughter back.

Though he said nothing about it to the men he had recruited, there was a secondary benefit to taking Victoria Westbury prisoner. When Choctaw asked her to go to the Cattlemen's Dance in Loraine, she had laughed at him. Laughed at him, as if he were nothing more than a saddle tramp. As far as Choctaw was concerned, a few days in fear and humiliation would be good for her.

Like his aborted plans to be a large rancher, however, that plan fell apart. Just when things were going well, the Crocketts came along—quite by coincidence—and rescued her. Now the Crockett brothers were the fair-haired boys at the ranch. They, and not he, were the ones Robin Westbury turned to when he wanted something done.

Choctaw had seen the way Victoria Westbury looked at Will Crockett. What did she see in him? He had no better background than Choctaw did. Hell, Will Crockett was a bushwhacker. He had ridden with Quantrill, and everyone knew that Quantrill's Raiders were the wildest and most savage group of men ever to fork a horse.

As far as Choctaw was concerned, Will and Victoria could have each other. It was time to move on. It began to fall apart when the Crocketts killed the four men Choctaw had recruited to abduct Victoria. They had been good boys, and they deserved more than to be shot down like mad dogs.

Percy was a good man too, and he deserved better, but Choctaw had had no choice. He hadn't wanted to kill Percy, but Percy had caught Choctaw rustling red-handed and was going to tell. Now things were really getting out of hand since Dan Berriman had introduced hoof-and-mouth disease onto the range. When Choctaw heard what Berriman was going to do, he cautioned him against it, but Berriman didn't listen.

"No, it's perfect if you think about it," Berriman had said. "One cow put into one isolated herd, and he'll have to destroy every cow on his ranch. That's the law. And there's no way anyone, not even someone as rich as Robin Westbury, can sustain that kind of loss. He'll wind up losing his land for taxes, and I'll pick it up for a song."

"If you ask me, you're grabbin' a bull by the tail and you might not be able to let go," Choctaw had warned.

Choctaw was right. Berriman's plan had backfired. Not only did Westbury not have to destroy every animal on his ranch, but Berriman wound up losing nearly as many of his own cattle. And so did several of the other ranchers.

But, like they say, every cloud has a silver lining, and Choctaw had just found the silver lining to this cloud.

He had come here to see Berriman, to "raise the price of playing poker."

Choctaw's musings were interrupted when, behind him, he heard the front door open and close. He turned to see Berriman coming out onto the porch.

"What are you doing over here, Choctaw? I told you never to come to my house. This isn't very smart of you," Berriman growled. "What if someone saw you?"

"I was very careful," Choctaw said. "I came through the hidden pass. Nobody saw me."

"That doesn't matter. It's not a good idea for you to be seen here. Especially now, with everyone so jittery over this hoof-and-mouth thing."

"That's all your own fault, Berriman. I told you not to do it," Choctaw said. "But you went ahead and put that sick cow in with Westbury's herd anyway, and look at all the trouble it's caused."

"Well, I guess it turns out that you were right. I didn't expect it to get out of hand the way it did. I thought it would be confined to Camelot. Instead, I wound up havin' to destroy over five hundred head of my own cattle."

"I can replace those cows for you," Choctaw offered.

"I'm sure you can, and I'm counting on it," Berriman said. He smiled. "And the best part is, the compensation I'm getting for destroying my cows will pay for the replacements. So, if you look at it that way, I'm still way ahead."

Choctaw shook his head. "Well, maybe not quite as far ahead," he said.

"What do you mean? I'm getting five dollars a head for every animal I destroy. And I'm paying you five dollars a head for every cow you bring me. It all comes out in the wash."

"Well, that's what I want to talk to you about. From now on it's gonna cost you ten dollars a head to replace 'em," Choctaw said.

The smile left Berriman's face and he looked up sharply. "Ten dollars a head?"

"Ten dollars a head," Choctaw repeated.

"You're gettin' a little greedy, ain't you?" Berriman asked.

"I don't call it greedy," Choctaw said. "I call it smart."

"Uh-huh. And what makes you think I'll pay ten dollars a head?"

"Because you need them cows, Mr. Berriman," Choctaw answered.

"You're still getting' 'em at a bargain rate, and there ain't no place else you can get 'em, 'cept from me. Besides which, you've got no choice. You have to do business with me."

"What do you mean, I have to do business with you?" Berriman asked.

" 'Cause if you don't..." Choctaw paused for a minute

and studied the hat he was still turning in his hand, then he cleared his throat. "Well, I just might have to tell some folks how that diseased cow got into the Camelot herd."

"I wouldn't want you to do that, Mr. Ford. That would make things very unpleasant for me," Berriman said.

"Yes," Choctaw said. "Yes, it would, wouldn't it?"

"Well, Mr. Ford, you have certainly given me something to think about," Berriman said. "Yes, indeed. I may just have to change the way I do business with you."

Choctaw nodded, then put his hat on, walked out to the hitching rail, and mounted. "I thought you might come around to my way of thinkin', Mr. Berriman," he said from the saddle.

"I haven't yet, but I'll think it over, and I'll send you my answer soon," Berriman promised.

"Don't make me wait too long," Choctaw said, gaining some confidence now. "I'm sure you wouldn't want me talkin' to the wrong people."

"No," Berriman said. "I wouldn't want you talkin' to the wrong people."

Choctaw jerked his horse around, then rode off.

Berriman watched Choctaw until he was out of the gate, then he started toward the guest house to talk to Sampson. When Berriman had hired Sampson he figured, rightly, that such a person wouldn't do well in the bunk-house with working cowboys, so he offered him the guest house. Sampson accepted the offer as if it were his due, though in truth it seemed that he rarely spent his nights there. Sometimes Berriman would see Sampson riding out toward town, just before dusk. Then he would see him coming back the next morning at dawn. He didn't know where Sampson went during those times, nor did he ever inquire.

Last night was such a night. Sampson had ridden out just after supper, and Berriman saw him coming back just after breakfast. Did he have a place to stay in town? Or had he spent the night outside, in the rain? Berriman was curious about it, but he wasn't curious enough to ask questions. As long as Sampson was around when he needed something done, then he served his purpose. Berriman certainly had no further use for him.

He did have a use for him now, though, so he stepped up onto the porch of the guest house and knocked on the door.

A moment later Sampson opened the door.

"My God, what happened to your face?" Berriman asked when he saw the four deep scratch marks down Sampson's left cheek.

"I got scratched," Sampson answered without elaboration.

"I'll say you did."

"You needin' me to do somethin'?" Sampson asked.

It was obvious he didn't care to talk about the scratches on his face and, therefore, Berriman didn't mention them again.

"Yes," he said. "I have a little job for you."

As Choctaw rode back toward the pass that would allow him to go from Double-Diamond to Camelot, he began making plans. They were happy plans. He already had twenty-five hundred dollars put away from his earlier business with Berriman, and if he brought him five hundred more cows at ten dollars a head, that would be five thousand dollars more. He would have to split with Rad, of course, but he would tell Rad that they were still getting five dollars a head, so Rad's share would only be one thousand two hundred fifty dollars. That would leave Choctaw three thousand seven hundred fifty dollars to add to the poke he already had. With that kind of money he could go anywhere and live like a king. Maybe even California.

Half an hour after he left Berriman's house, he heard someone coming after him. When he stopped and turned around to look, he saw that it was the lipless creature who worked for Berriman.

"Well, now, I see it didn't take Berriman long to make up his mind," he said aloud. He chuckled and reached down to pat his horse on the neck. "What do you think, horse? Looks like me an' you's about to be in some pretty tall cotton."

Sampson pulled up about ten feet away from Choctaw.

You are one ugly son of a bitch, Choctaw thought, though he didn't give voice to the words. Then he noticed the four long, red marks on Sampson's left cheek, and realized that they were scratch marks.

"Ha, look at them scratch marks!" Choctaw said. "What'd you do, run into a wildcat who didn't want anything to do with you?"

Sampson put his hand to the scratch marks for a second, then lowered it.

"You might say that," he said.

"Oooweee. Seems to me like that's more woman than you can handle. If I was you, I'd stay away from her."

"I'll do that."

"So, what are you doin' out here? Were you coming for me?"

"Yes."

"Berriman sent you?"

"Yes."

Choctaw smiled broadly. "Yeah, I figured he'd see things my way. What did he tell you?"

"He told me to kill you."

The smile froze on Choctaw's face. For just a moment he wasn't sure he'd heard what he thought he heard.

Then he thought it must be some sort of joke, though it was a joke that made his skin tingle.

"That... that ain't funny," Choctaw said nervously.

"No, I don't reckon it is," Sampson replied. He pulled his pistol and pointed it at Choctaw.

"What the—" Choctaw shouted. "No, wait! Wait! Tell Berriman I was just—"

Sampson pulled the trigger and the slug caught Choctaw in the center of his chest, right in the breastbone. It hit with the impact of a hammer, and Choctaw felt all the breath leave his body. He put his hands over the entry wound, then looked down to watch in horror as his own bright red blood began spilling through his fingers. He tried hard to stay in the saddle, but lost the struggle when Sampson fired a second time. That bullet hit Choctaw right between the eyes.

Chapter Nineteen

Douglas Poole was not only a lawyer, or "barrister," as Westbury liked to say, he was also the father of two school-aged children and the president of the Loraine school board. When Miss Martha Jane Stevens resigned her position to get married, Poole was charged with the responsibility of finding a replacement teacher. It was Robin Westbury's recommendation that Poole hire Miss Mollie Vitters for the upcoming school year.

"Mollie Vitters is an exceptionally bright young lady," Westbury had said, "and someone who is at ease with responsibility. And she is also a very pretty young woman, as you shall soon see. I don't think the school board will have any regrets."

"I would hope she is not too pretty," Poole had replied. "Miss Stevens was rather plain, yet even she managed to get married. The pretty ones don't last long at all. Sometimes they get married in the middle of the school year, and if that happens, we are left in a terrible fix."

Poole, with the approval of the school board, hired Mollie Vitters for the upcoming school year. Classes would be starting on Monday morning, and last week Mollie had moved into her room behind the school. She had spent the entire previous week getting ready.

Shortly after Mollie arrived, she gave Douglas Poole a list of repairs she wished made to the school. One request was that the roof be repaired, and, because of the heavy rain yesterday and last night, Poole decided to go over to the schoolhouse today to see for himself how badly the roof leaked.

He was surprised to find the front door of the school standing wide open. He climbed the steps, then stuck his head in through the door.

"Miss Vitters?" he called. "Miss Vitters, it is I, Douglas Poole. Did you intend to leave the door open?"

When Poole got no response from his call, he took another few steps into the schoolroom. "Miss Vitters, are you here?" he called. He looked around the room and saw several books lying on the floor.

"My word," he said. "What is all this?"

Miss Vitters had only been here a few days, but already Poole had been impressed with her neatness and organization. It certainly wasn't like her to leave books lying around. How strange, he thought.

"Miss Vitters?" he repeated.

Poole moved farther into the room. Something was wrong. Something was terribly, terribly wrong.

"Miss Vitters?" Poole called, his voice louder and more urgent.

Poole moved to the front of the classroom, which was actually the back of the school building. When he reached the first row of desks, he saw something that had been previously blocked from his view by those same desks. There on the floor halfway between her own desk and the blackboard lay Mollie Vitters.

"My God!" Poole gasped.

The teacher was lying on her stomach. Her head was turned to one side, and her eyes were open and unseeing. Her right arm was outstretched, and a piece of chalk lay on the floor beside her hand.

Will and Gid were fitting pipe to one of the wells when Mo rode up.

"Hi, Mo," Gid greeted with a smile. He took in the well with a wave of his hand. "What do you think? We'll have this one going by the end of the day. That will give Camelot five working wells."

"Yeah, it looks good," Mo said. His voice was low and solemn.

"What is it?" Will asked. "What's wrong?"

Mo took a deep breath. "Don't know no way to say this, other'n to come right out an' say it," he began. "Gid, you know that girl that was here for a while? The Vitters girl?"

"Mollie, yes, what about her?" Gid asked.

"Well, Gid, I hate to be the one to tell you this, seein' as how I think you was maybe a little sweet on her."

"What is it, Mo?"

Mo took his hat off and ran his hand through his hair.

"They found her dead this mornin'," Mo said. "That is, Lawyer Poole, he found her dead."

"What? Where? How?"

"She was layin' right there on the floor in the school-house. She was shot."

"Oh, damn," Gid said with a long, breath-expelling sigh. "What kind of a bastard would hurt a sweet girl like that?"

"Have they caught the one who did it?" Will asked.

Mo shook his head. "They don't even know who did it," he said. "But whoever it was, his name starts with a C."

Gid looked up in interest. "His name starts with a C? How do you know that?"

" 'Cause before she died she wrote the letter C on the floor of the school," Mo explained. "They figure she must've been trying to write the name of whoever did it, but that there letter C is as far as she got."

Gid started for his horse. "I'm going into town, Will," he said.

"I figured you would."

Gid mounted, then looked back toward his brother. "Well, you comin' with me, or not?"

"I'm comin'," Will replied.

Jasper Haynie, the town undertaker, had learned his trade during the war. He became so skilled at restoring battle-damaged soldiers to a state to be viewed by their grieving family members that he achieved a well-deserved degree of fame. Now, when he had a project of which he was particularly proud, he would display the body on a catafalque just inside the big glass window on the front of his funeral home.

He was particularly proud of the job he had done with Mollie Vitters. He had fixed her face into a slight smile, used rouge and lip paint to restore some color, and combed her hair so that it lay in soft curls around her face.

Since her uncle was killed just a short time earlier, Mollie Vitters had no family to view her. Haynie thought it would be a shame to let such a wonderful job pass without some recognition, so he lay her body in his most beautiful coffin, a black lacquer box with silver scrollwork. Then, folding her arms across her chest, he placed a single yellow rose in her hands and put her on the catafalque in the front of his establishment.

Word began to spread around town that Mollie's body would soon be on display. As a result, a crowd gathered outside the window. Some were friends, here out of genuine grief. Some were mothers and fathers of the children Mollie was to have taught, and they were here out of respect. But a sizable number had gathered from unashamed curiosity.

As if opening the curtain on a staged drama, Jasper Haynie pulled back the drapes so his work could be seen. Then he stepped outside, beaming proudly, as he listened to the accolades for his work.

"Oh, look how beautiful she is," someone said.

"Doesn't she look natural?"

"The color's good. Just like she's sleepin'."

When the Crockett brothers arrived at about that time, they saw the crowd gathered around Haynie's front window, and they rode over to see what everyone was looking at. They were startled to see Mollie's body, and, because Gid didn't want to see her this way, he jerked the horse away quickly.

"Let's get the hell away from here," he growled.

"Good idea," Will agreed. "What do you say we go down to the saloon and have a drink?"

"Yeah. Well, I'll be there in a couple of minutes," Gid

replied. "First, I want to go down to the schoolhouse and have a look around."

"All right," Will said. "I'll see you in a bit."

When Gid reached the school building, he saw two men, wearing badges, standing out front. He dismounted and started inside.

"Where do you think you're a'goin'?" one of the deputies asked.

"Inside," Gid replied, pointing to the door. "I want to see where she was killed."

"Mister, you want to gander, you go down there with the rest of 'em and look through the window at Haynie's. They got the little lady on display down there. No need in your hangin' around here. There ain't nothin' to see."

"Wait a minute, Bill," the other deputy said, when he noticed the pained look on Gid's face. "Did you know her, mister?"

"Yes," Gid answered without elaboration.

"Come on, Bill. Let him go on inside, it ain't goin' to hurt nothin'."

"Froggie, you heard what the sheriff said, same as me. He said, don't let nobody mess up what she wrote on the floor."

"We'll go inside with him," Froggie suggested. "He won't mess nothin' up."

"What's your name, anyway?" the deputy called

Bidge asked.

"Crockett. Gid Crockett."

"Crockett?" Bidge replied, putting his finger alongside his nose. "Is that Crockett with a C or with a K?"

"C."

"That's interestin'," Bidge said. "Come on inside, and I'll show you why."

Gid and the two deputies went into the empty school building. Bidge pointed to a chalk mark on the floor. "We figure she must've been tryin' to tell us who killed her," he explained. "Only thing is, she died before she could get it writ. All she could make was the letter C. Like the C that's in your name," he added pointedly.

"You think I did it?"

"Nope," Bidge replied easily. "If I thought you done it, I'd have my gun out an' pointin' at you by now. But I know you didn't because," he put his hand to his face, "you ain't marked up none."

"What do you mean?"

"It seems that when Mr. Haynie examined the girl's body he found blood and skin under her fingernails. He reckons Miss Vitters must've put up a pretty good fight before she was shot."

"Sure would like to get my hands on the son of a bitch who did it," Froggie said.

"Yeah, me too," Bidge agreed. "I'll tell you one thing,

if we do catch him and a crowd gathers outside the jail to lynch him, I sure as hell ain't goin' to be the one that fights 'em off."

Gid thanked the two deputies for letting him look around, then rode over to the Cattle Call Saloon. He tied his horse off at the same hitching post Will used so that the horses, used to each other by now, would stand quietly side by side, then he went inside. Will was already at the bar, and Gid went over to stand beside him. The bartender put a mug of beer in front of him before he could even speak.

"I already ordered, and I told him to be on the lookout for you," Will explained.

The two brothers, their drinks in their hands, turned their backs to the bar and looked out over the other patrons. It was pretty clear what the conversation was about. Everyone was talking about the "beautiful young schoolmarm," who was found on the floor of the school-house. And there were as many speculations as to what happened to her as there were speculators.

Gid was just finishing his beer when Sampson pushed his way into the saloon through the batwing doors. His entrance had an immediate chilling effect on the patrons, and though all conversations didn't stop, they did grow much less animated.

"I wish that son of a bitch would find some other place

to do his drinkin'," the bartender growled. "Ever' time he comes in here, my business drops off."

"Why?" Will asked.

"Don't you know? That's Jude Sampson. He's the one killed them two cowboys from the Cripple C, for no reason a'tall. He just up an' picked a fight with 'em, then shot 'em down in cold blood."

"We were told it was a fair fight," Will said.

"Fair fight? Look at him, the way he wears his guns kicked out like that," the bartender replied. "You think anyone could get the better of him in a fair fight?"

Sampson stood in the door for just a moment, looking over the patrons in the saloon, then he turned and walked over to the far end of the bar. The patrons who had been standing there moved away, giving him a wide berth. That was when Gid saw his face. And what he saw made him draw in a quick, audible breath.

"What is it?" Will asked quietly.

Gid didn't answer. Instead, he dipped his finger into his beer, then began marking on the bar. First he made the letter C. Then he made the letter S. Then he started to make the letter S, but he didn't complete it. Instead, he let his finger tail away. The result was a mark that looked exactly like the chalk mark Mollie had left on the floor over at the school.

"Son of a bitch!" Gid said under his breath. "It isn't

a C, it's an S!"

"What are you talking about?"

"The mark Mollie left on the floor. Ever'one thinks it's a letter C. But it's not." He pointed to his own effort, which was already beginning to dry up. "It's an S that she couldn't finish, just like that one."

"S? Sampson?"

Gid nodded. "Look at his face. The deputies said she scratched whoever did it. He did it, Will. There's not a doubt in my mind. Sampson killed Mollie Vitters."

Gid started toward Sampson. Anxious for him, Will reached out to put his hand on his brother's shoulder.

"Easy, Gid," he said. "You've heard the talk about him. He's damned good with that gun. I'm not sure I could even handle him."

"You won't have to handle him," Gid replied quietly. "I'll do it."

"Gid?" Will started anxiously, but paying no attention whatever to his brother, Gid went over to stand beside Sampson.

Sampson, not used to being crowded, looked up.

"Step back, you big bastard," he said. "I don't like bein' crowded."

"Did you kill Mollie Vitters?"

"What?" Sampson asked, not only surprised by the question, but surprised that anyone would have the nerve to ask it.

"Mollie Vitters," Gid repeated. "Did you kill her? Is that how you got those scratches on your face?"

Sampson put his hand to his cheek. "I got these here scratches by ridin' through some brambles," he said.

"You're a lyin' son of a bitch, Sampson. Mollie scratched you when you killed her."

"You can't prove that."

"Prove it? I don't have to prove it, you ugly-assed bastard. All I have to do is believe it."

No one had ever challenged Sampson like this, and there was a collective gasp of breath as everyone started paying close attention to the conversation between Gid and Sampson.

"Mister, I'm going to count to three," Sampson hissed. "If you ain't gone by then, you'd better be drawin' your gun, 'cause I'm going to blow a hole through your innards."

By now, even those who had gone upstairs had somehow learned what was going on, and several of them came to the railing on the second-floor landing. They stood there, like patrons in a theater, looking down on the drama that was playing out at the bar. A few looked at the clock to note the time. They would need all the facts for their telling and retelling of the story over the years.

"Start counting, you runty little son of a bitch," Gid said.

Now not only conversation but breathing stopped

as everyone waited, silently, to see what was going to happen. The loudest sound in the room was the measured tick tock of the pendulum clock that stood on the side wall between the piano and a brass spittoon.

An evil smile spread across Sampson's lips. He liked the old adage: The bigger they are, the harder they fall. This son of a bitch was big, and he was going to fall like an oak tree.

"One," Sampson started.

Gid didn't flinch.

"Two ... three ..." At three, Sampson drew his pistol. He expected to see Gid going for his own gun, but Gid surprised him. Instead of attempting to draw against Sampson, Gid stuck his hand out and intercepted Sampson's hand as it came up.

This was the same hand Sampson had wrapped around the handle of his pistol. It was small, delicate, and graceful. ... all desirable attributes for someone who wanted to learn the skill of rapidly drawing and firing a pistol.

But the pliant fragility that was an advantage to the skilled shootist now became a shortcoming. Gid squeezed his big hand down on Sampson's small one.

"Hey, what the hell?" Sampson shouted.

Gid squeezed hard, so hard that Sampson's fingers began breaking one by one.

"Ahhhh!" Sampson screamed in pain as he felt his

fingers snap under Gid's viselike grip.

The evil and confident smile on Sampson's face was instantly replaced by an expression of pain and surprise.

Gid began to raise Sampson's hand. Sampson had no idea what Gid had in mind, but he was powerless to prevent it. Sampson's gun hand came up, then twisted around backward. As the muzzle of his own pistol was brought around to bear on his face, Sampson's expression of pain and surprise turned to one of awareness and horror.

"No!" Sampson screamed. "No, what are you doing?"

At that moment it became impossible for him to speak further, because Gid rammed the barrel of Sampson's own pistol down his mouth. He thrust the gun barrel so far down Sampson's throat that Sampson started gagging.

That was when Gid pulled the trigger.

Chapter Twenty

The gleaming coach and four stood on the curving drive-way in front of Westbury's house. The driver stood on the ground beside it with the door open. Will and Gid, their horses saddled, were waiting as well, for Westbury had asked them if they would go into town with him.

"You're certain you don't want to ride in the coach?" he asked as he started to get in.

"No, thanks," Will replied. "I feel closed up in those things."

Westbury chuckled. "A bit of claustrophobia, eh? Well, I suppose I can understand the condition, though, believe me, it is much more comfortable riding on a padded seat than sitting on a hard saddle."

"I'll grant you that," Will replied.

"I want to thank you two men for going to see the federal inspector with me," Westbury said. "You can give him a firsthand report on the disastrous effect that Gypsum River dam has had."

"We'll be glad to tell him our story, Mr. Westbury," Will said. "But I don't know how much attention a Yankee government official is going to pay to the likes of us."

"Oh, he'll pay a good deal of attention, I should think. Especially when he learns that Gid is a water engineer."

Gid laughed. "A water engineer, am I? Well, I would've never called myself such a thing."

"And why not? Have you, or have you not, located and dug five producing water wells?"

"Well, I've done that, I reckon," Gid agreed.

"That, my fine friend, makes you a water engineer," Westbury said. Just before he got into the coach, he saw Mo giving some of the cowboys their instructions for today. "Still no sign of Mr. Ford?" he asked.

Will shook his head. "I've checked around," he said. "No one has seen hide nor hair of Choctaw in nearly a week."

"How very odd that he should just disappear like that," Westbury said.

"That's the way it is with some men," Will said. "When they get the urge to move on, that's just what they do."

"Yes, well, I do wish he would have had the common courtesy to tell me that he was leaving. That way I could've found a new foreman."

As they were talking, the cowboys who had been

instructed by Mo started to ride away. One of them stopped and called a question back to Mo. Mo answered it to the cowboy's satisfaction, and the cowboy nodded, then rode on.

"Seems to me like you've already found your new foreman," Will said. "Mo seems to be running things better'n Choctaw ever did."

Westbury had been watching Mo as well, and he nodded. "Yes, I am quite pleased with the way Mo has stepped in and taken over. I think you might be right about him," he agreed.

Westbury got into the coach and the driver closed the door, then climbed up onto the high box that was his seat. With a whistle and a snap of the lines, the team lurched forward and the coach began to roll out of the driveway, the gravel making a crunching sound under the steel-rimmed wheels.

When they reached town, they went directly to the law offices of Seely, Hamilton, and Poole. Douglas Poole met them on the front porch, then they all went to lunch at Mabel's Cafe.

"Mr. Shackelford is due to arrive at two o'clock," Poole explained over the lunch table. "We will meet his train and talk to him long enough to make our grievances known, then we'll go see Condon."

"Do you really think you're goin' to get any satisfaction from a damned Yankee official?" Gid asked.

"This Yankee is from Washington," Poole explained. "It is to be hoped that we would get a fairer judgment from him than we would from some carpetbagger."

"Like that pissant Condon, you mean?" Gid said.

"My point exactly," Poole replied. "If Condon has been unduly influenced by the likes of someone like Dan Berriman, then we have recourse in the court system."

A small man wearing a three-piece suit and glasses which were supported not by earpieces but by perching on the end of his nose stepped down from the train. A gold chain stretched across his vest, and he pulled his watch out and examined it.

"Would you be Mr. Benjamin Shackelford?" Poole asked, stepping up to the arriving passenger.

"I am, sir. And you would be Mr. Condon?"

"No, I am Douglas Poole. I represent Mr. Robin Westbury and some of the other area ranchers."

"Ah, yes," Shackelford replied. "You are the lawyer who has filed a petition to halt the water improvement project."

"Yes," Poole said, "but I am also the lawyer who requested the water improvement project in the first place."

"Mr. Poole, you must realize that a government project is rather like a steamboat paddling down a river.

Once it is in motion, it takes a great deal of effort to stop it, or to turn it around. So, tell me, why the change of heart?"

"The dam," Poole said.

Shackelford looked confused. "The dam? What dam? We authorized no dam."

Poole and Westbury looked at each other in surprise, then Poole turned back to Shackelford.

"Are you telling me that the government did not authorize a dam to be built across Gypsum River?"

"Heavens no. Why would we do that?" Shackelford asked. "I've studied the maps. A dam across Gypsum River could create water deprivation for the entire range."

"It not only could, it has," Poole said. "For indeed, Mr. Shackelford, a dam has been built."

"Does Mr. Condon know about this?"

"He certainly does, Mr. Shackelford, for he's the one who built it," Westbury said.

Shackelford took his glasses from the end of his nose and polished them furiously for a moment, then he put them back on.

"Gentlemen," he said, squaring his shoulders. "I suggest we go speak with Mr. Condon at once. If what you are telling me is true, he has some explaining to do."

During the walk from the railroad depot to Condon's office, Poole told Shackelford about some of the water problems the range had been facing lately, and how those problems had been exacerbated by the dam across Gypsum River.

"The problem has been somewhat alleviated by the engineering genius of Mr. Gid Crockett," Westbury put in.

"Oh? And what has Mr. Crockett done?" Shackelford asked.

"He is getting water from underground," Westbury said.

"I see. You have located and identified the aquifer, then?"

"The what?" Gid asked.

"The aquifer... the underground source of water. I thought you were an engineer."

"I never said that," Gid said.

"Then how did you find the water?"

"I witched it, with a dowser," Gid said easily.

Shackelford laughed. "You found the water by dowsing for it? How quaint."

"It might be quaint, Mr. Shackelford, but Camelot now has five good wells and is much less dependent upon Gypsum River. Still, the dam must be removed if the other ranchers are to get their fair share of water."

At that moment they reached the district water office. The door was standing slightly ajar, and Shackelford pushed it open.

"I shall be interested in hearing what Mr. Condon

has to say about this," Shackelford said, stepping into the office. "Condon?" he called. "Mr. Condon, it is Benjamin Shackelford, from the Department of the Interior. Are you here?"

There was an eerie silence to the office, and the four visitors stood there for a moment, waiting for Condon's reply.

"He should be here," Shackelford said. "I am absolutely positive he knew that today was the day I was to arrive."

"He knew it," Poole said. "We were talking about it last night." The lawyer pushed through a little spring-loaded gate that separated the front of the office from the rear. "There's a document storage room in the back," he said. "Perhaps he's back there."

"If what you gentlemen have told me about the dam is true, it's going to take more than a few documents to justify his action," Shackelford said, pushing through the gate to follow Poole to the back.

Poole opened the door, then stopped short, with a look of surprise on his face. "I'll be damned," he said.

"What is it, Douglas?" Westbury asked.

Poole stepped back, then pointed toward the open door. "Condon is in there," he said.

Knowing that something was wrong, Will, Gid, and Westbury moved through the little gate to join Shackelford, who was also now looking through the door, his mouth open in surprise.

There, hanging from a rafter, twisting slowly at the end of a rope, was the body of Harris Condon.

Will, Gid, Westbury, Shackelford, and a United States marshal were riding out to the dam. There, Shackelford would order the sluices opened immediately, thus providing a source of water for all the ranches downstream. Then he would make the determination as to whether or not the dam itself should be brought down.

There was no longer a question about the legality of the dam. Condon's suicide note explained it all. He told how he had accepted money from Berriman to use the water improvement project to both enrich the Double-Diamond and to impoverish all the other ranches.

The letter also gave one piece of additional information, information which Will and Gid could scarcely believe.

"In the interest of truth, and the hope that such disclosure will, somehow, make amends for my own transgressions, I would also inform you that the man you know as Dan Berriman is in fact Jonas Perkins, late a captain in the Federal Army. A few months after the war ended, Captain Perkins stole an army payroll with which he had been entrusted, and deserted. That stolen payroll provided the money he needed to start his ranch."

"Jonas Perkins?" Will said in surprise.

"You have heard of him?" Westbury asked.

"Yes," Will said. "If it is the same one, I have heard of him."

"Will, how can it be the same one?" Gid asked. "The Jonas Perkins that we know is dead."

"Is he?" Will asked.

"You know he is," Gid said. "We killed him."

"We thought we did," Will agreed. "But, if you recall, we didn't stay around long enough to make certain. We never saw his body."

"We didn't have to see the body. How could anyone live through something like that?"

"We did, Little Brother," Will replied easily.

Gid was silent for a long moment, then he nodded. "Yeah," he said. "Yeah, that's true, isn't it? We did live through it."

"From the tone of the discussion you two are having, I gather that you know Berriman from before," Westbury said.

"I don't know," Will answered. "We knew a Captain Jonas Perkins. But the man we knew sure didn't look anything at all like Berriman."

"You are no doubt talking about his lack of hair," Westbury said. "He explained that to me once. It seems that, during the war, he was caught in a terrible explosion. The effect of the explosion was not only to burn off all the hair on his head, but also to destroy the follicles that grow hair."

"Son of a bitch," Will said. "It *is* the same one. It has to be."

"Tell me about him," Westbury said, riding alongside them, the better to hear the story.

Will explained that Jonas Perkins had been a captain in the Federal Army, and a particular adversary during the war. As provost marshal for Kansas City, Captain Perkins was the one who was charged with the responsibility of rounding up Quantrill and all of his Raiders, including men like Bloody Bill Anderson, George Todd, Frank and Jesse James, the Younger brothers, and Will and Gid Crockett.

But Quantrill and his Raiders were proving to be too elusive for him, so Perkins decided to give himself some leverage. He did that by rounding up all the wives, sisters, mothers, daughters, and sweethearts of the men fighting for the South and putting them in a makeshift prison over a liquor store in Kansas City.

The conditions in the women's temporary prison were as harsh as any prisoner-of-war camp in the country. In addition, there were no provisions made for the fact that these particular prisoners were of the "gentler" sex.

The women were watched over by armed guards, publicly humiliated, and physically mistreated. And, when a tornado struck Kansas City, Captain Perkins made no effort to move them to a safer place. As a result, many of them, including Bloody Bill Anderson's sister and a girl Gid was particularly fond of, were killed when the building in which they were housed, was destroyed.

Later, when the war was over and Gid and Will, responding to a general offer of amnesty, turned themselves in, Captain Jonas Perkins took it upon himself to deny them the parole that had been granted to everyone else. It was his intention to take personal charge of Will and Gid, and to escort them to St. Louis where he planned to publicly hang them.

But Perkins underestimated the ingenuity of the Crockett brothers. In a daring escape, the boys ignited a keg of gunpowder which was being carried on the same train that was transporting them to St. Louis. Railroad regulations directed that both the prisoners and the powder be carried in a special car attached to the end of the train.

The explosion not only separated the car from the rest of the train, it blew the car apart. Will and Gid, who were in the rear, managed to duck down behind the seats and thus avoid the blast. Then, with the car blown free from the train and in smithereens about them, they were able to get away.

Captain Jonas Perkins and the escorting guards were

in the front part of the car during the explosion. Until today, Will and Gid had thought the guards and Perkins had been killed in the blast. It would appear, however, that somehow Perkins had survived.

Berriman was standing at the sluice gate when they arrived. Word had already reached him that Condon had committed suicide, and Berriman reasoned, correctly, that there would be a note implicating him. He jacked a shell into his rifle and held it out in front of him.

"That's far enough," he called. He was smoking a cigar, and he pulled the cigar from his mouth to use as a pointer. "You can just turn around and go on back to town."

"Mr. Berriman, this gentleman with us is Benjamin Shackelford," Westbury said. "He is a representative of the Federal Department of the Interior. He has come to order the sluice to be opened so that the water may flow."

"I don't give a damn if he's the President of the United States," Berriman replied. "Nobody is going to touch my dam."

"Oh, so it has become *your* dam now, has it?" Westbury asked. "Well, I am glad you have given up the charade of saying it was a project backed by the government."

Will rode up a little closer, in order to get a really good look.

"I'll be a son of a bitch," he said. "Gid, it's true. It is him."

"You mean he *is* Captain Perkins?" Gid asked.

"Yes," Will replied. He looked at Perkins. "Do you remember us?"

"The Crockett brothers. You may as well ask me if I remember Quantrill, George Todd, or Bloody Bill Anderson. In fact, I have even more of a reason for remembering you two bastards," Perkins said. "You thought you killed me, didn't you? You left me there to die. Only I didn't die. Instead, I came out looking like this."

Perkins waved his hand in front of his face, then laughed. "At first, I was angry. But later, it proved to be a blessing in disguise. When I stole the payroll money they posted a reward for Jonas Perkins. But Jonas Perkins no longer existed, you see. He really *did* die in that train explosion."

"Mr. Perkins, it's all over for you now."

Perkins shook his head. "No," he said, "I told you, Perkins is dead. Don't you know who you are talking to? I am Dan Berriman. I am one of the biggest ranchers in the state of Texas. Why, I can buy and sell people like you!"

"No you can't, and that's the point," Shackelford said. "I have already taken steps to have the federal government confiscate your ranch. And you, Mr. Perkins, are going to prison for robbery and for bribing a government official."

"Step aside, Perkins," the U.S. marshal called. "Step aside so we can open the sluice gates."

"You want the sluice gates open?" Perkins said. "I'll accommodate you."

Perkins twisted around and touched the lit end of his cigar to a fuse.

"I'm blowing this dam all to hell! You want water? You'll get water!" Perkins shouted.

A quick glance around showed Will the danger they were in. They were in the dry riverbed, but just on the other side of the dam was a lake, caused by the pooling of the river. When the dam went, a thirty-foot-high wall of water would come crashing down on them. Here, the sides were too steep and too high to get out. It was at least fifty yards back down the riverbed before the sides sloped gently enough to allow them to exit.

"Let's get out of here!" Will shouted, turning his horse around even as he called the warning.

Perkins began laughing hysterically. "Run! Run, you lily-livered bastards! Run!"

Will sensed his brother to one side of him. To his surprise, Westbury managed to get ahead of them, taking his horse over obstacles as easily as if he were running on a road. The marshal was just behind, and Shackelford was behind the marshal.

The blast went off then. Will felt it before he heard it—a pressure wave that washed over him from the rear like a hot, desert wind. Shortly after that he heard it, a deep-throated roar as loud as any explosion he had ever experienced during the war.

He reached the sloping sides of the riverbed and with the slightest touch turned his horse. The horse responded quickly and within a few bounds they were out of danger.

Turning back toward the riverbed he saw the wall of water crashing down through the channel, knocking down trees, sweeping up debris, tumbling and swirling with so much energy that even the banks of the river were caving in.

Shackelford's horse stumbled as it started up the side and he was thrown over its head. Gid, who was the closest, darted down to him, then leaned over from his saddle, reached down, and, with one hand, was able to snap the small man up. He rode back to the safety of the others, just as the water came crashing through where Shackelford had been. Shackelford's horse wasn't as lucky, and Will saw its eyes, wide in terror, as it was swept helplessly downstream.

After the water went down, its level lowered by the fact that it was now furnishing water for the entire valley, they found Perkins's body. It was lying on the side of the river, half in and half out. His neck was broken.

Gid and Will stood just over his body, looking down at it for a few moments, then they climbed back up the bank and mounted their horses. Westbury and the others had already started east, toward Camelot, and were at least a quarter of a mile away by now. The Crocketts looked in their direction.

"Will, did you leave anything back at the ranch?" Gid asked.

"Nothing I can't replace," Will answered.

"Which way?"

"West."

"Sounds good to me."

A Look At: Showdown At Red Rock (The Crocketts' Western Saga: Six)

A five-star masterpiece from best-selling author Robert Vaughan.

Will and Gid are looking forward to a quiet rest in the tiny town of Sulphur Springs. But Will's female companion offers more than he bargained for when she says her brother was murdered by outlaws. It's more than the marshal can handle, but word is that the Crockett brothers can.

AVAILABLE NOW

About the Author

Robert Vaughan sold his first book when he was 19. That was 57 years and nearly 500 books ago. He wrote the novelization for the mini-series Andersonville. Vaughan wrote, produced, and appeared in the History Channel documentary Vietnam Homecoming.

His books have hit the NYT bestseller list seven times. He has won the Spur Award, the PORGIE Award (Best Paperback Original), the Western Fictioneers Lifetime Achievement Award, received the Readwest President's Award for Excellence in Western Fiction, is a member of the American Writers Hall of Fame and is a Pulitzer Prize nominee.

Vaughan is also a retired army officer, helicopter pilot with three tours in Vietnam. And received the Distinguished Flying Cross, the Purple Heart, The Bronze Star with three oak leaf clusters, the Air Medal for valor with 35 oak leaf clusters, the Army Commendation Medal, the Meritorious Service Medal, and the Vietnamese Cross of Gallantry.

www.ingramcontent.com/pod-product-compliance
Lightning Source LLC
Chambersburg PA
CBHW011434240626
47153CB00011B/2988